THE PAINTED PENNY STAMP

FRAN SMITH

HOG FEN

*O*n a grey afternoon in early November, Miss Hazelton, white-haired, hatless and with her coat flapping around her, rushed along Eden Street and knocked frenziedly on the door of number 144. A hint of the under-cloud light that comes before dusk lit her anxious figure as she called through the letterbox and pounded on the door.

Vita, roused from her desk, hurried to answer.

'Oh, Miss Carew! Come quickly!' Miss Hazelton gasped, clutching at Vita's hands. 'Come quickly. It's Mr Flett. He's had an accident. Something dreadful.' The old lady tugged Vita out of the door.

ALBERT FLETT LAY on his back in the attic room he used as a study. A dark pool of blood surrounded his head, soaked like a ragged halo into the rug. Vita's first aid training told her to check his pulse and listen to his chest. She found no breath, no pulse, no movement. His hand and cheek felt cold.

'We must send for a police officer, Miss Hazelton. There's nothing to be done for him, I'm afraid.'

The old lady sank into the room's only armchair, wringing her handkerchief. 'He ate supper with me only yesterday. Poor Albert. Oh, poor dear boy. How could this have happened?'

'Does he have relations?' Vita asked gently. 'Anyone we should inform?'

'He always said he was alone in the world, poor thing.'

They both looked back at the figure of the young lodger. He was neatly dressed, his suit well brushed, his collar crisp and white, his shoes well-polished. Even the soles of his shoes were clean.

It looked as if he might wake at any moment, Vita thought, as if he might sit up and smile and return to his work. But they both knew that would not happen.

A pounding step on the stair heralded the approach of Constable Williamson, who entered with his helmet under one arm. The maid had found him on his beat.

'You have checked for signs of life?' he said. The constable and Vita had been to first aid classes together.

'Yes. I found none present, but please check for yourself.'

Williamson set his helmet on the desk and knelt to do so. The women watched, hoping for a miracle.

'No. I shall have to record that life was extinct upon my arrival at - he checked his pocket watch - at four forty pm,' Williamson declared. He stood and wrote in the notebook he drew from his pocket. 'Your maid tells me this gentleman is your lodger,' he said to Miss Hazelton.

'He is. His name is Albert Flett. He has lived here for over two years. Lovely young man, he is. *Was*, I should say.' Miss Hazelton gasped and wiped another tear.

'I shall need to examine the body further now. It might be wise to wait downstairs,' the constable told Miss Hazelton.

Miss Hazelton's maid-of-all-work, Agnes, appeared in the

doorway. She was a solid, middle-aged woman in an apron. She glanced with a frown at the body before leading Miss Hazelton firmly out of the room. 'I'll get the mistress of cup of tea,' she said. 'She'll be in the parlour if you need her.'

Alone, Vita and the constable continued to examine the body. They rolled it over to reveal a head wound—a considerable indent in the back of the skull.

'That's what finished him. I'd say he tripped on the fender, fell backwards and hit his head on the mantel shelf,' Williamson said. He looked around the room. 'I've seen it before in these little attic rooms. A big marble mantel shelf with a hard edge like this. Catch yourself wrong on it, and this happens. I'd have the edges rounded off on every mantel shelf in the country if I had my way.'

He examined the corner of the black marble shelf and pointed Vita's attention to a blot of what appeared to be blood on its sharp corner.

'Poor fellow,' Williamson said. 'The fire wasn't even lit. Not that a grate that small would give you much to warm yourself by.'

It was true. The mantel shelf was heavy marble, but the fireplace beneath was so small that it had barely enough room for a handful of coals. A mean little fireplace in a room intended for servants.

'I shall have to report to the Inspector, this being a fatality. I can't say that I see anything suspicious to report, though. It looks like an unlucky accident to me.'

The constable took out his pocketbook and began making notes. Vita looked at the surroundings. It was a comfortably furnished room. Flett had placed his desk under one of the dormer windows. Pens and coloured pencils, paintbrushes and ink bottles were ranged in orderly ranks along a single shelf nearby. A sketchbook lay on the desktop. Williamson flicked through it, revealing landscape drawings and a few pages of calligraphic lettering.

'Do you know what work he did, Miss?' he asked Vita.

'He was a commercial artist. I believe Miss Hazelton mentioned he worked for one of the big department stores in London designing advertising posters.'

'You knew him, Miss?'

'Not well. I saw him once or twice in the street. I feel I know him because Miss Hazelton was always talking about him. He was the best of all lodgers. She was always singing his praises.'

Williamson said nothing, but began opening drawers and looking along the bookshelf before moving across the passageway to the small bedroom opposite. That, too, was fastidiously tidy. Spare boots, polished and paired, stood against the wall. A coat and a hat hung on a hook. The bed was made with folded-in corners. Williamson put his hand into the pockets of the greatcoat and brought out a wallet. It contained four shillings and four pence in coins. Williamson wrote all this in his notebook.

A clatter and a stomp came on the stairs. The maid returned. She held a bucket, its water steaming and soapy, and a mop. 'I want to get that stain out,' she said, nodding toward the blood on the rug. 'The sooner I get to a stain like that, the better. Blood can be the very devil to get out.'

'I can't allow it,' Williamson said. 'Not until my Inspector has observed the scene exactly as it is.'

Agnes looked put out. 'He don't need to see the stain. You can just tell him about it. Where's the harm in a clean carpet?'

'Did you hear any noises earlier today? It must have made a noise when he fell,' Vita asked, to change the subject.

'I was in the basement doing a bit of ironing. I wouldn't

4

hear anything from the attic. And Missus is getting deaf, so she heard nothing.'

'No callers came to the house today? No visitors to Mr Flett?'

'Not today. He sometimes 'as a visitor, but no-one came in lately.'

'Can a visitor come up here without you knowing?' asked the constable.

Agnes seemed irritated by that idea. 'Who'd open the door? The mistress never hears the bell. I always answer the door myself.'

'Is there no back door, or tradesman's entrance?' the constable persisted.

'There is a side door, but no back stairs. If someone was to come in that way, they'd have to go up to Albert's room by the main stairs and I should see them.'

'Even if you were ironing in the basement?' asked the constable.

Agnes's face was turning red. She was finding the young constable's questions irksome. His manner offended her dignity as much as the bloodstain drying on the rug offended her sense of orderliness. 'The mistress has sent for the under-taker. I hope your Inspector won't be long. I can't abide mess on a carpet.'

It was growing dark outside. Before carrying her bucket and mop away, Agnes lit the lamps in the room and drew the curtains. As she did so, the light fell on a postcard that had fallen into a corner. Williamson reached for it and held it under the lamp. On the front was an old-fashioned engraving of King's College chapel. The constable glanced at both sides, then passed it to Vita with a shrug. She was examining it when Inspector Llewellyn thundered up the stairs.

'You are a witness?' the Inspector asked Vita. He was a

tall, stout man who occupied a lot of space in the small attic. His voice was deep and booming, more suited to addressing ranks of officers standing to attention on a parade ground than two people in the enclosed space of Albert Flett's rooms.

'I am a neighbour,' Vita said. 'You and I have met before, Inspector, in the hospital. And once at the police station after a misunderstanding on the train from Littleport.'

Llewellyn prided himself on his memory. He narrowed his eyes, summoning Vita's face from his mental filing system before nodding. 'Miss Carew. I remember now. So this unlucky chap is your neighbour, is he?'

Llewellyn strode into the attic sitting room and looked the body over from a distance. 'You have checked the underside?' he asked his constable.

'Blow to the head, Sir. Bloodstain on this corner of the mantel shelf.' Williamson was standing at attention, awed by the arrival of the high-ranking officer.

Llewellyn peered at the shelf. 'Well spotted, Williamson. And your conclusion?'

'An accident, Sir. An unlucky accident. I believe the gentleman tripped on the hearth rail, or stumbled on the edge of the rug, and fell backwards. His head hit the corner of the mantle shelf at an awkward angle, and that was enough to kill him.'

'Suspicious circumstances?' boomed the Inspector.

'None that I can see, Sir.'

'He has a bruise on his jaw,' Vita said suddenly.

Both police officers bent over the body. A faint blue patch could be seen under the skin along the dead man's right jawline.

'I didn't see that before,' said the constable.

'It wasn't there before,' Vita told him. 'It's developed since we have been here.'

Llewellyn raised an eyebrow. 'Ah yes. You're studying science. I remember that now, Miss Carew. Make a note of the alleged bruise, Williamson. I shall send the police surgeon to certify death. See what he thinks of Miss Carew's bruise ideas. I'm still inclined to think it was an accident. It's likely he hit his jaw on the way down.'

'The maid says there were no visitors,' the constable added.

'I shall have a word with her myself,' Llewellyn said. 'There's no need for you to stay, Miss Carew. You can follow me down.'

VITA'S AUNT Louisa insisted they both drink a small sherry before she heard the news about Miss Hazelton's unfortunate lodger.

'Inspector Llewellyn believes it was an accident and Constable Williamson agreed with him,' Vita said, after explaining the scene. She could feel the sherry making her face red already. 'They say he tripped on the hearth. His injury suggests he caught his head against the sharp corner of the mantel shelf.'

'You sound doubtful. You are not convinced of that your-self?' her aunt asked.

'Perhaps I am too suspicious.'

Her aunt smiled and sipped the golden sherry. They were sitting beside the fire. There was a trace of oil paint—it looked like Payne's Grey—on the back of her hand. She had spent a good deal of the day on a portrait of a senior college organist, a man so colourless that the wallpaper behind him was in danger of looking more interesting than he did. 'Your suspicions do often lead to something, dear,' she said.

CHAPTER 2

*V*ita pulled the postcard from Flett's room from her pocket and examined it. 'This caught my eye. It was on the floor. There's something odd about it, but I can't quite put my finger on what it is.'

Louisa Brocklehurst glanced over her niece's shoulder. The postcard had a print of King's College chapel on one side and Flett's own address on the other. The message read *hoc signum arte* and was signed *H.B. Longbridge.*

'What can it mean?' Vita asked.

'The Latin just means *this is a sign of my work,* said her aunt. Perhaps this H.B. Longbridge drew the image on the front.'

'Have you heard of an artist by that name?'

'Longbridge? The name rings a bell, certainly. I shall have to think about it. I must go now, and dress for dinner. I am invited to High Table at King's. The Master is hoping for news of their organist's portrait, no doubt. I have an idea that they are testing my skills before deciding to commission portraits of one or two other senior men. It could be a very promising line of work. Would you care to join me? I could easily arrange an invitation for you, Vita.'

'I have an anatomy examination in a few days.'

'Is this the one your senior tutor insists you pass?'

'I'm afraid so.' Remembering the tense interview with Miss Ledbetter, the famously fearsome scourge of first year science students at Newton College, made Vita flinch. She tucked the postcard back into her pocket and headed back to her desk. She tried to concentrate but her thoughts kept wandering back to Albert Flett, so dead in his tidy room, the bruise developing on his jaw.

VITA CALLED on her other neighbours, the Goodmans, early the next day. Mrs Goodman opened the front door but turned immediately and called over her shoulder, 'Georgie, I've told you once. Do not jump from the fourth stair. It is far too high. You will break a leg.'

'But that was only the *third* stair, Mama,' the boy replied in the background, picking himself up off the floor. He was four years old, the youngest of the five Goodman children.

'No arguments! Stop that immediately and go upstairs to Ginnie, she is waiting with your medicine.'

Mrs Goodman turned back to Vita as the boy stomped upstairs. 'I do apologise, Vita,' she said. 'The boy was up half the night, weeping and wailing about something he saw in a dream. Are you looking for Charles? He is working on an invention in the conservatory. Do come in.'

Dr Goodman, with sleeves rolled up and a brown wood-worker's apron on, was nailing one end of a long strip of rubber to a plank of wood. 'Ah Vita,' he said. 'Come and see the Muscle Enhancer.'

Vita looked politely at the construction, but how it would enhance anything was not plain to her at all. 'How does one...?'

'It's very simple. It is designed to offer repeated practice in flexing the muscles of the arm. One pulls on the India rubber strip. It resists strongly, and so the muscles of the arm are forced to work harder; this improves their strength. I am convinced it will be a very popular device as soon as I iron out one or two little problems.'

'It broke my best mirror yesterday,' his wife remarked.

'Well, yes. The rubber came loose at one end.'

'And a plant pot the day before.'

'I admit,' Dr Goodman said, 'that there have been one or two technical difficulties. Mainly in securing the rubber strip to the wooden panels - it tends to split.'

'Vita did not come to hear the details of the Enhancer, Charles. At least, I don't think so.'

'You heard about Albert Flett?' Vita asked.

'Yes. Miss Hazelton called this morning. Very unfortunate. You saw him, I heard.'

'Yes. It was a wound to the head and he was quite dead when I arrived. There was one odd thing, though. A bruise to his jaw.'

A thud and a shriek from the hallway caused Mrs Goodman to rush out of the conservatory. Her husband ignored it, looking quizzically at Vita instead. 'You are not sure it was an accident?' he asked.

'The bruise was barely visible, but it seemed to develop during the time we were there. After he was dead, that is. Is that possible?'

'Yes, that can happen. Why are you concerned about it?'

'I couldn't see how he would have a new bruise to his jaw

after he had fallen backwards against the sharp edge of the mantel shelf. It didn't make sense.'

'But the police were satisfied that he had just fallen?'

'Yes.'

Goodman thought about this for a moment as he finished his nailing and began testing the strength of the join. 'There will be a post mortem, of course.'

'Yes. The police surgeon will carry it out today, they said.'

'The police surgeon?'

'Yes. Do you know him?'

'I know him well. Underhill. A figure of some renown.'

'I was wondering whether I might persuade him to let me be present? Perhaps with your help? I have attended dissections in my university class and been present at the photographing of a post mortem.'

Goodman wrapped the rubber strap around his fist and pulled against the join he had just made. The effort made him speak through clenched teeth. 'Underhill's work is distinguished, but he is notoriously short-tempered – cantankerous, some say. I saw him box an undergraduate's ears once in a forensics lecture. Stalked off the stage and caught him a whallop for not paying attention. He does allow undergraduate observers at his post mortem examinations, but he is reputed to dislike women students. I will send him a note but I shall neglect to mention that you are female. You should do the same. But Vita, beware of doing anything to offend Underhill. He is an influential man. People on the wrong side of Underhill rarely thrive, to put it plainly.'

He gave one last firm pull on the rubber band, which split, catapulting its inventor several feet backwards into a potted palm. Vita was relieved that plant and doctor both escaped harm this time.

11

Young Georgie was sitting on the bottom stair alone when she passed on the way out. Even looking gloomy, he was the loveliest of the Goodwin children. His mop of golden curls had yet to be trimmed into anything more boyish, and his sisters often dressed him as a girl. Today, though, he was wearing blue knee britches and a jauntily blue and white striped shirt, giving the overall impression of a very small French sailor.

'Nobody believes what I say. It's because I am the littlest,' he sighed as Vita passed. She sat for a moment beside him.

'I'm sure I'll believe you, George. What was it about?'

'I saw a nasty man kick Minmou,' he said. Minmou was a neighbour's tabby cat, a great friend of George's, and amiable enough to approach everyone who passed in the street, purring a welcome.

'When did you see that?'

'In the middle of the night. I heard a noise and looked out of the window. Minmou was sitting on the wall. A man came past and she went to see him, but he just kicked her. He kicked her up into the air. I heard her cry.' Tears were welling in the boy's eyes at the memory.

'I'm sure Minmou was not hurt, Georgie.'

'I looked for her this morning. She always comes to our gate, but she did not come to visit today,' said the boy. The tears now rolled down his cheeks and he caught his breath in a muffled sob. 'I couldn't see her anywhere.'

'I will look on my way home. She is probably just resting in her own house. I promise I will look very thoroughly.'

'He was a nasty man,' George said.

'He was, but I expect Minmou will just be resting. Cats are strong creatures.'

'It wasn't a dream. Everyone thinks it was a dream,'

George said, cheering a little now he had been heard. He looked up and wiped his tears away on his sleeve.

'I shall check that Minmou is well, and as soon as I find her, I shall come and tell you,' Vita told him. 'But don't jump too far down the stairs, will you?'

'Only three, not four?'

'Only three.'

'Alright,' the boy agreed, with a shrug.

Vita hurried across Eden Street and wrote immediately to Dr Underhill, saying she was an undergraduate, but not mentioning that her college was a women's college and carefully signing herself V. Carew, in the hope he would assume she was a male student, and therefore admissible.

On the way back from the letter box, she made a long and thorough check of the walls and gardens all around for signs of the little cat, but found none.

The reply came in the half past two delivery. '*Dear Mr Carew, We begin at 4pm sharp. Theatre 3, Old School Lane. You will not be admitted if you are late. F. Underhill FRCS, Police Surgeon, Cambridge Constabulary.*'

CHAPTER 3

The operating theatre used for post mortems was familiar to Vita. It was on the top floor of the laboratory building, up a set of winding stone stairs. Vita wore a dark jacket and skirt, hoping to be inconspicuous, and followed a lively group of young medical students up, planning to slip into the room at the back, somewhere that would offer her as much invisibility as possible. Several of the professors were unwelcoming to women students, so this was her usual practice when attending lectures.

Dr Underhill, in a rubber apron with his shirt sleeves rolled to the elbow, entered at the same moment the body was wheeled in. The police surgeon was a tall man in his fifties.

On the stretcher the corpse was and was not, Albert Flett, Vita thought. It was transformed, as were all the bodies she had seen, by its pallor, its nakedness, its stillness. It was a young man, his life cut short, but it was also a peaceful presence. Corpses show no regrets. They have already accepted their fate.

Brisk and efficient, Underhill began by uncovering the body and walking around the table making general observations. A departmental secretary, a grey-bearded gentleman Vita had seen at work before, wrote them in shorthand. 'We observe here the body of a healthy young man in his late twenties or early thirties,' Underhill said. 'He is approximately average height.' Two orderlies, with a tape measure, followed the professor. They applied it to the body, showing him the reading. 'That is to say, five feet four inches tall, and we know already that he weighs a little under eleven stones.'

'I shall begin as usual, with my summary of external observations.' The professor moved around the body, leaning in to inspect something with particular attention here and there. 'There are no scars or outward signs of ill health on the front of the body. The teeth are in good order. The finger nails on both hands are clean and undamaged.' Leaning over the head, the professor added, 'The one exception to this is bruising to the right jaw.' The professor took a magnifying glass and a short ruler from a table. 'It comprises a patch one and three-quarter inches wide and three quarters of an inch high. The bruise is darker at the sides and lighter in the centre.' The professor set his magnifying glass down and turned to the students. 'This is the type of bruising we often connect with what, gentlemen?'

He looked at the half dozen students expectantly. His eyes falling on Vita without reaction.

'It might indicate a punch,' one of the young men in the front row suggested.

'Yes. Why?' asked the professor, turning back to the body.

'The two lighter patches might be where the bones of the knuckle made contact, Sir.'

'Well done, Parker. Wake up the rest of you. Yes. This kind of bruising is characteristic of a punch to the jaw. In this case, the punch of a right-handed attacker, where the first two knuckles of the assailant's hand do the damage. I'm told that people in the fighting game - bare-knuckle fighters, for example - avoid this kind of punch. It damages the hand. The trained fighter aims to strike with the flat of the clenched finger bones...' the professor turned again and held his clenched fist up to the students, showing them what he meant. 'By avoiding the knuckles, a fighter inflicts injury whilst protecting his own hand.' He turned back to the body, pointing to the bruise on Flett's jaw. 'This, then, if indeed it is a punch, is the punch of an amateur. Someone who lost his temper and lashed out without thought of the damage he might do to himself or the victim.'

The men around Vita expressed interest in this observation. The police officer in the front row wrote in his notebook. All were impressed.

'But could this injury, or a very similar one, be inflicted by falling forward, onto patterned ironwork, for example?'

The question was out of her mouth before Vita had time to stop herself. The professor spun round. Everyone in the room, including Vita, held their breath.

Underhill considered Vita's question. He frowned. 'Why do you ask?'

'There was a fire surround which had a patterned wrought ironwork edge in the room where he was found.'

'Yes, I do believe there was,' said the Police Surgeon. He turned back to the body and scrutinised the bruise on the jaw once again. 'Well, I would need to see it again, but I prefer the punch explanation. And there would be the question of his falling forward onto his jaw, when the wound to the back of his head was inflicted, as far as the police observer could tell - and he has evidence of a bloodstain - by falling backwards against the corner of a marble mantel shelf. No, on balance I would suggest this man was punched hard but inexpertly, and that the momentum of the punch threw his head backwards onto the jutting marble shelf. If he fell forward, the marks on his face would be different. They would be less likely to be on the jaw, for example, and more likely to be across the cheek or nose.'

Vita nodded. Several of the surrounding men glanced over, wondering whether she was about to receive one of Underhill's cutting remarks, but none came.

'Turn the body over,' he instructed the porters. The two men rolled Albert Flett's remains over, and the dark hole in the back of his skull was revealed. The hair had been shaved around the deep indentation that had killed him. Underhill continued his superficial observations for a few minutes, noting again the unscarred and apparently healthy skin and limbs, before making his first cranial incision and revealing the fractured shard of bone that had penetrated the brain and probably ended the victim's life.

'This young man was exceptionally unlucky,' Underhill remarked. 'The bone of his skull is - I shall need to confirm this by measurement later, but my suspicion is that the density of his skull is fractionally thinner than average. The blow he received, on a normal skull, would have caused injury, but it would probably not have been fatal. The angle at which he fell and the sharp point of the mantel shelf were such that the skull broke on impact and unfortunately for him, the bone...' Underhill reached as he spoke and with his pincers held aloft a sharp triangle of skull bone. It was the shape of an arrowhead. '... fractured in an unusual way and was driven deep into his brain. A catastrophic combination of factors which ended his life. A slightly different angle, a slightly less sharply carved mantel shelf, a slightly thicker density of bone, and he might have survived.'

'What would cause such a thinning of the bones of the skull?' Vita asked.

Underhill dropped the shard of bone into a waiting dish. He kept his back to the students, continuing his examination of the wound. 'That is not a question for the post mortem, although it is of interest. Perhaps one of your more senior colleagues would care to suggest some possible causes?'

The students around Vita rustled and shuffled anxiously for a moment, before one of them said, 'It can be inherited. But it's usually idiopathic.'

Underhill now turned to them. 'Yes. In other words, we have no satisfactory explanation, but we favour a medical-sounding term to conceal the fact. It is one of many examples of a condition that only an unusual set of circumstances reveals. In this case, he could have lived a long life without ever knowing his skull was an eggshell, but he was unlucky.'

Vita was the last to leave after the post mortem was concluded. She was deep in thought about what she had just seen and did not care to be caught in the bustle and press of young men hurrying away. A forensic post mortem, with its painstaking thoroughness, its intensive focus on finding the cause of a death, its methodical measuring, weighing, note-taking, was impressive - theatrical, almost. It had taken almost two hours to establish that Albert Flett, healthy and without disease in the major organs of his body, had fallen against a mantel shelf, which would have caused most people a nasty bump and a headache, but which was sufficient to kill him. The bruise to the jaw was noted. No certain connection could be made between it and the fatal injury.

Two orderlies were tidying the room now that the body had been returned to the mortuary. They were piling instruments into trays for cleaning, folding the cloths used to cover the body, mopping the floor. For the first time, Vita noticed that the sharp, metallic smell of blood was in the air.

'This would not be a very comfortable place to spend the evening. I imagine you have warmer and more welcoming places to go to.' It was Dr Underhill. He had returned for the cuff links he had left on a shelf, and found Vita alone.

She stood hastily. 'Thank you for allowing me to attend,' she said.

Underhill looked at her coldly. 'I do not usually permit young women. Medical students are distractible enough without them. Women are attracted to medicine for the caring and curing. Generally, they have little time for the cutting up of corpses.'

Vita began to leave.

'What did you make of the post mortem? It is your first, I assume.' He spoke briskly, rolling down his sleeves and fastening the gold links into the cuffs.

'I have dissected and been present at the photographing of a body after a post mortem examination, but yes, this is the first time I have observed the whole procedure.'

'You found it revolting, no doubt. Messy and unpleasant.'

'Not at all. I found it awe-inspiring.'

Underhill looked up from his left cuff, where the link was giving him trouble, and watched curiously as Vita left.

CHAPTER 4

'I knew the name Longbridge was familiar,' Aunt Louisa said. She was in her studio the next morning, arranging it for her sitter's arrival.

'Longbridge?' Vita had just returned from an early search for the missing cat.

'Longbridge. The name on the postcard. It came to me this morning. I used to know a Lady Henrietta Longbridge through the Ladies Lecture Society. She lives in an enormous house along the Chesterton Road. A great castellated place with brick pillars. Probably the largest and certainly the ugliest house in Cambridge. Her father built it on the proceeds of a fertiliser manufacturing fortune. I believe it was he who acquired the title. I met Lady Henrietta several years ago. She was far from young then. She must be in her eighties by now. Quite a character.'

'A wealthy lady, then?'

'Oh yes, she makes no bones about that. She inherited her father's fortune and, if I remember rightly, that of several unmarried uncles, too. She never married. She still gets about, I see her occasionally in a wheeled bath chair. I saw her going into Waring and Pilkington's on Castle Hill only last week. She was always very eccentric. I remember her wearing a beautiful Turkish rug to meetings. She cut a hole for her head and wore it as a sort of tabard. It was an unusual costume, even for Cambridge.'

'Waring and Pilkington's?'

'They are solicitors. Even years ago, she had a reputation for constantly changing her will. Almost every week, a maid would do something to offend her and have to be struck out of it. Or she would develop a fancy for a new charity and decide the Potters' Benevolent Society or a Donkey Sanctuary in Inverness needed a few funds. A difficult woman, certainly, but I suppose she had charitable instincts, at least.'

Louisa turned back to the empty chair waiting for her sitter. 'Now, I'm hoping to bring a spark of life into the organist's eyes today. I have here a list of topics of conversational topics. I am determined to enliven the man. Something must be done. He is inclined to sit there like a sack of potatoes.'

Vita glanced at the list. It read: *magic, marmalade, mountains, music.*

'How did you select these topics, Aunt? They seem an unlikely combination.'

'I threw open the dictionary. I am desperate. I have never painted anyone as silent and distant. He is a waxwork! And my painting will look like the portrait of a waxwork unless something can be done.' She threw the green cloth over the sitter's chair, arranging its drapery with care. 'By the way, Dear, Miss Hazelton asked if you could call round this morning. Agnes needs help with moving poor Mr Flett's possessions.'

. . .

MISS HAZELTON, wearing mourning clothes for her lodger, opened the front door to Vita herself. 'Ah Vita, my dear. How kind of you to come. You find us very sad today.' She led Vita to her front parlour and invited her to sit.

This room, like most of Miss Hazelton's house, was filled with a lifetime's collection of dried flowers, lace doilies, ornaments, statuary, painted fans, portraits, porcelain animals, watercolour landscapes, blossomy rugs and tasseled draperies.

'He was a dear boy, you know. The very best of lodgers. His visitors came and went like mice, and he kept those rooms as neat as a pin. Quiet, tidy, polite. And good company too. He often joined me for dinner. He told me all about Bainbridge's. He knew the latest fashions; the decorations at Christmas. He described the window displays. I felt I was there. I truly did. I shall miss him dreadfully. Poor, poor boy.'

'And he has no family that you know of?'

'None that he ever mentioned, no. He was alone. I think that may be why he took to this household. I truly believe Agnes and I were like family to him. But what are we to do with his belongings? Who should we contact? We are uncertain. Agnes is clearing his rooms, but what to do with his things? I told her to box them up for now. Poor boy. I shall have to ask Mr Waring what one does in such terrible circumstances.'

'Mr Waring?'

'My solicitor - lovely man, always a rock in times of trouble.'

The old lady shed a few tears, dabbing her eyes with a lacy handkerchief. 'I wonder, Dear, if I might ask you a great favour? We need to clear the rooms because, well, not to be too blunt about it, the rent is my only income. Agnes is not as young as she once was. There are one or two cupboards she cannot reach into. And between you and me, I think she dislikes being up there alone. I wonder whether you could spare a little time to help her?'

IF SHE WAS anxious about being alone in Albert Flett's former rooms, Agnes showed it by attacking her cleaning duties with double her usual vigour. Vita found her scrubbing the floor-boards on hands and knees in a headscarf and long apron. She was just finishing the sitting room, backing out, before starting on the bedroom. A different, clean hearth rug lay where the bloodstained one had been.

'Miss Hazelton said you might need a hand to reach some of the cupboards, Agnes,' Vita said.

The maid pushed her hair away from her face with the back of her hand. Her face was flushed with the effort of scrubbing. 'Yes, Miss. There's a cupboard runs all round the eaves. It goes into the roof space. I can't reach the back of it without climbing right out into the roof. I don't like to, not with my bad back.'

Most of Flett's belongings were already packed into his suitcase and a pair of tea chests. The room being in the attic had a steeply sloping ceiling, the flat part of the wall behind the bed being only about three feet high. Agnes pointed to an inconspicuous door handle there. When she opened it and peered in, Vita saw a wide roof space that could be used as an extra cupboard. Pushing her head through to look round, she could see that boards had been laid over the joists, making it easy enough to climb into the space. She was shocked by how cold it was up there, but the explanation soon became clear. In one corner, right at the furthest angle of the roof, there was a sizeable gap in the slates. Daylight flooded in, along with the icy wind. Vita crawled over and found a pile of slates lying beneath the opening. Leaning as far as she dared, she could see the nails that would have held the missing slates were twisted and bent at odd angles, as if they had been wrenched aside.

'Are you there, Miss?' Agnes called.

Vita clambered back to the opening into the attic bedroom. 'There's a hole in the roof here, Agnes. Have you noticed it before?'

'An 'ole? No, Miss.'

'It'll need mending urgently, Agnes. The rain will get in. It doesn't seem damp yet, but that far corner is open to the elements.'

'The wind must've blown off a few slates, I expect.' Agnes slid the trunk and the tea chests up to the entrance to the loft and Vita hauled them through. There was plenty of room. She stowed them well away from the hole. Peering round, she spotted what appeared to be a folded blanket tucked into a dim corner. She had to lie at full length along the rafters to retrieve it.

Opening the bundle back in Flett's room, revealed an artist's sketchbook and a small, dog-eared exercise book. The sketchbook had an undecorated black cover and would have contained about fifty pages of fine quality paper. When she opened it, Vita found it contained only five empty pages, the others having been removed, leaving only a row of tidy cut edges.

Vita remembered something. 'Agnes, when you opened the door to Mr Flett's callers in the past, did any of them give you a name?'

'One of them was called Brown,' Agnes said. 'A rude man, always complained I was slow to open the door. Didn't like to be kept waiting.'

Vita picked up the exercise book and opened that. Each

page was filled with line after line of closely written notes, dates, places, figures. In contrast to the sketchbook, which was pristine and carefully kept, the little exercise book was frayed along the edges and looked as if it had been carried about. Notes were in different pens and sometimes carelessly written. The pages curled as if it had often been thrust, rolled, into a coat pocket.

'That, Miss, is a form book,' Agnes said.

'A form book?' Vita did not know what she meant.

Agnes sighed and sat heavily down on the bed. She shook her head. 'I knew there was something. I should've guessed.'

'Guessed what, Agnes?'

'The thing is, Miss, I don't want to upset the Missus any more than she already is. She thought Albert Flett was 'er very own little angel from heaven, she really did. She could see no wrong in 'im because he was kind, polite and so on, but I was never so sure about 'im.'

'You disliked him?'

'The Mistress is as innocent as a lamb, Miss. She's never 'ad a bad thought, not once in all her long life. She only sees the good in people. She's easily fooled because of 'er sweet, innocent nature, if you see what I mean.'

'Do you think that Albert Flett was doing something wrong?'

'I don't know what he was doing. I only know 'e didn't tell the truth. He was supposed to go to London for his work, but I've passed the station more than once and seen 'im waiting for a Newmarket train.'

'Perhaps he was visiting a friend.'

Agnes shook her head. 'Newmarket is where the horse racing goes on, Miss. And the betting besides.'

'But Mr Flett worked in one of the great department stores in London, didn't he?'

'Perhaps he did once. He liked telling the Missus about it, but - I don't know about big London shops, Miss - but to me it all sounded like fairy stories. The Missus couldn't get enough of it. She used to shop there at Christmas when she was young. It brought back good memories for 'er. She loved Albert to describe the decorations and the wonderful things they sell there. The pair of them spent whole evenings talking about it.'

Vita looked again at the blue exercise book. 'You said this was a form book?'

Agnes made a sour face. 'For the races. Racing people, people who follow the gee-gees, they make notes like that. I grew up in Newmarket. My brother works for a trainer. E's got one like that.'

'So Mr Flett studied the horse races? But why?'

'They do it to know which one to put their money on. For gambling, Miss. For betting on the 'orses.'

Agnes sounded as if she was explaining to a child. Rather a slow child.

'This might be important, Agnes. You must give these things to the police when they return.'

'They said nothing about returning,' Agnes said.

'Even so. You should tell them about these, and where we found them.'

Agnes looked into the distance for a moment, then sniffed. 'It might be better coming from you, Miss. The police are not interested in what a maid-of-all-work has to say. What difference does it make, anyway? Albert Flett's dead and gone. What if he did waste his money on the 'orses? It'll only make the Mistress grieve even more, if she finds he was not the nice young man she took him for. Where's the good in that? Her 'eart is not good. All this upset is bad for 'er.'

It was easy to see that this was true. 'I think these should be taken to the police, anyway,' Vita told her.

'Well, you take them, and I won't worry the Missus until the police decide what it all means, Miss. I think that's for the best.'

Vita agreed and carried the books back to her room. On the way, she looked for the little cat, as she usually did. There was still no sign. The professor who owned Minmou had not seen her either. Vita wished she had some good news to tell Georgie. And meanwhile there was a great deal more revision to be done on the anatomy of the hand and wrist.

CHAPTER 5

*L*ouisa poked the fire. Wearing her paint-stained apron, she was cleaning brushes. Winter sunlight flooded in from a clear blue sky, but the room was still bitterly cold. She wore fingerless gloves and a woollen shawl. 'Come in, Dear. Mr Pottendale left early. The life of a college organist is busier than one would imagine.'

She removed the cloth covering the portrait she was working on and stood glaring at it with her hands on her hips. 'Oh dear. That face should express musical genius. So far, it expresses only vacancy and boredom. It won't do at all. The Master is eager to commission further portraits of at least four or five senior Fellows, but only if I can impress them with Mr Pottendale here. This is the portrait of a potato.'

She sighed and turned to Vita. 'Forgive me, Dear, I have not asked how you found the post mortem on poor Mr Flett.'

'It was fascinating. There is a possibility that he was punched shortly before he hit his head.'

'Good Heavens! Punched by whom? What do the police say? Didn't Agnes tell you there were no callers?'

'The police do not find the evidence of any interest,

apparently. Agnes says she let nobody in, but she also says she was in the basement doing the ironing.'

A knock was heard, and Vita left her aunt to examine the portrait. In the hall she met Ginnie, the Goodman family's nursery nurse, led up from the back door by Tabitha. She stood awkwardly in the hall as Vita was called.

'I'm sorry to trouble you, Miss, only Master Georgie is in hysterics. I can't calm him. He saw something - a man - in Fitzroy Street just now. And just let out a shriek. I had to hold him back. He tried to follow the man - and - I'm afraid he tried to kick him! He keeps saying he must speak to you. I'm ever so sorry to bother you, but we can't settle him.'

'I'll come immediately, of course.'

They found Georgie sitting on the stairs, surrounded by doting sisters. He had stopped howling, but was still tear-stained and shuddering with sobs.

'Here is Vita now, Georgie. She has come. Tell her what you saw,' Ginnie told him.

The boy was still breathless and juddery, but said quietly. 'The man. The man who kicked Minmou. I seed him. It was him. The same man.'

Mrs Goodman shooed her daughters away. 'Give the boy some room, girls. Back to the schoolroom now.'

'You're sure it was him?' Vita asked, sitting beside George on the stair.

'Yes. I know it was him. The same man. The same nasty man.' The boy's chin was wobbling again. Vita patted his hand.

'Did you see this man, Ginnie?'

'Yes, Miss. He was coming out of Norman Bradley's shop.'

'Which shop is that?'

'The pawnbroker's, Miss. It's about half way down. The one with iron bars over the windows.'

'What did he look like?'

'Very tall, lanky, dark-haired. And foulmouthed. Swore like a trooper.'

'Because Georgie was making a noise?'

'Well, he kicked him in the ankle, too. Before I could stop him.' The nursemaid looked embarrassed and added. 'It was my fault, Madam. I should have been quicker.'

Mrs Goodman waved her apology aside. 'It sounds as if the bounder richly deserved a kick. Don't apologise, Ginnie.'

'I shall go to the shop and see if they know who he is,' Vita said.

'Give him a kick from me, if you find him,' said Mrs Goodman, 'there was no call for foul language. He is clearly no gentleman.'

THERE WERE no customers in the shop when Vita arrived a few minutes later. A bell rang and a thin-faced man with a sandy moustache and darting eyes appeared behind the counter as she entered. He was wearing an apron and had a pencil behind one ear.

'What can I do for you, Miss?'

Vita, having hurried, realised she should have planned what to say. She had heard of pawnbrokers, but never been in such a shop before and had little idea how they were run. 'There was someone here just now, a gentleman. I was wondering whether you could confirm his name,' she said.

The clerk narrowed his eyes. 'And why would you be enquiring about one of my customers, Miss?' The man had an insinuating and over-familiar way of speaking. Vita disliked it.

'I believe he left something behind when he visited a neighbour of mine,' she said, improvising.

The pawnbroker had a duster in hand. He ran it thoughtfully over the counter in front of him. 'And what was that gentleman's name, Miss?'

'Brown,' Vita said. 'That was the name he gave.'

'And what gives you the idea that it was the same gentleman?'

'My neighbour recognised him.' Vita decided to withhold the detail that the neighbour was four years old.

'A maid was it?'

Vita was reluctant to answer any more of this man's searching questions, but could think of no easy escape, so improvised again. 'Yes. Miss Hazelton's maid, Agnes Venner. She was the one who knew the name.'

Agnes' name caused a change in the man's expression. He looked around the shop for a moment, considering. 'I had the gentleman's silver hipflask in the window,' he said. 'He came in for it. But the name wasn't Brown.'

'He had pawned his own hip flask?' Vita asked.

The pawnbroker looked about again, as if to demonstrate that far stranger items than a silver hip flask were often pawned. 'Well-made little flask, that is. He'd have bought that in London. But no, as it happens, he didn't pawn it, he just dropped it in the street, and I, honest citizen that I am, picked it up and put it in my shop window so that the rightful owner could claim it.'

'And did he give a name, if it wasn't Brown?'

'His initials are on it, on a silver ring around the neck. Nice little object. Leather-bound. Proper gentleman's hip flask, that was.'

Vita was growing impatient. This man seemed to be playing some sort of game with her. 'And the initials were...?'

'I can't go giving out the names of my customers, Miss. That would never do, not in this line of business. Discretion is the name of the game in my work. That is why I am the foremost pawnbroker in the city. People rely on my discretion.' This was said in tones of moral superiority. He took up the cloth and began to polish a brass candlestick, breathing on it first, then polishing vigorously.

He is toying with me, Vita thought. 'So you do not feel able to tell me the initials?'

The pawnbroker folded his duster, smoothing it out. 'It would not be good for my business to hand out people's names.'

'Would you confirm the initials, if I gave them to you correctly?'

He looked away, into the back of the shop, then sighed. 'I suppose that would be acceptable, yes.'

'Were the initials HBL?'

The man raised his eyebrows and gave a grudging smile. 'They were.'

A thought came to Vita. 'How long did you have the hip flask? You found it when?'

'First thing in the morning - yesterday. I open at seven, so it must have been dropped in the night. The young gentleman was on his way back from a convivial evening, I imagine. You know what the young gentlemen from the colleges are like.'

Vita knew very well what gentlemen from the colleges and their convivial evenings were like. 'Was he a pleasant young man, this particular college gentleman?'

'I can't say he was. I'd say he was on the rude side. Just took his flask and left. A more generous man might have left a sixpence, considering I did the honest thing and took up space in my window with it, but not this fellow.'

'Well, thank you for your help.'

'You might tell Agnes Venner I've something here waiting for her, if you happen to see her, Miss.'

'Shall I say what it is?'

'That's for me to know and Agnes to find out,' he said, with an irritating wink, before taking the next candlestick down from the shelf.

CHAPTER 6

*M*iss Hazelton was making her way down Eden Street as Vita returned. She was a frail figure, leaning on her rolled umbrella and moving slowly.

'Are you going far, Miss Hazelton?' Vita asked. 'Shall I find you a cab?'

'Oh no, no, Dear. I'm quite well, thank you. I am going as far as Castle Hill, to the solicitor. I must ask him what to do with poor Albert's belongings. A cab will not be needed. The fresh air will do me good, I expect.' The old lady waved goodbye and continued determinedly. Vita looked after her. It was a damp day. A sharp easterly wind was whipping fallen leaves along the gutters. Miss Hazelton's slight figure was buffeted. She staggered as she tried to hold her hat and her umbrella at the same time.

'Perhaps I could walk with you, Miss Hazelton? If you would permit?'

Miss Hazelton was surprised by the offer. She protested a little, but Vita offered her arm and the old lady accepted it. They made their way slowly across town, the old lady finding some pleasure in the outing. She clearly left the house only rarely and saw much to interest her in the shops and people along the way. 'Do you care for fashion, Vita?' she asked, as they passed one of the dress shops. 'I used to be a great enthusiast for the Paris fashions at one time. My sisters and I - there were three of us - were good dressmakers. We used to buy the magazines and copy the latest designs. We were never wealthy, of course, but we were skilled at making over something from the year before. Adding a ribbon here, a lace trim there. Oh, we turned a few heads in our day! I was a red-head, just like you.'

Vita laughed to hear that. The old lady's hair was entirely white now, but on consideration, Vita could appreciate that her black mourning hat was rather elegant.

'Of course, I was never clever, as you are,' Miss Hazelton continued. 'I had very little schooling. It wasn't expected in those days. My father was a medical man, a pharmacist. He and mother expected us all to marry and have families. My two sisters did, but I was left at home to help care for them in their old age.'

Miss Hazelton did not sound regretful. They paused to admire a beautiful shawl in the window of a haberdashery. 'Albert told me the paisley shawls at Bainbridge's were exquisite. Indian designs, woven in wool, but soft as silk. A terrible price, they were, but the London ladies simply couldn't buy them fast enough. I shall miss his lively company. He dined with me twice a week, you know. I so loved hearing about Bainbridge's. A great department store is such a treasure trove of luxuries. He kept me up with the latest styles. I would ask him, *now Albert, what shape are hats to be next season*? And he would report back with all the details. He told me only last week that a softer, wider brim is favoured for next Spring, but I expect you know that already. Oh!'

Miss Hazelton turned suddenly, clasping Vita's arm. 'I suppose nobody has told them at Bainbridge's about poor Albert. I shall have to write to them. Another sad duty. I would travel to the shop myself, but I don't feel strong enough at present. Oh dear.'

'If it would help, it would be no hardship for me to take the train to Bainbridge's. My aunt would probably join me, she has been saying that she would like to do some shopping in London.'

'You are very kind. That would certainly put my mind at ease. They must be wondering where poor Albert could be.'

The realities of the lodger's death brought on a few tears, and the old lady was very low in spirits as they approached the office of Mr Waring, the solicitor.

The office was half way up the only hill in Cambridge, in an ancient timbered building next to Magdalen College. The flagstone pavement was blocked by an invalid's wheeled chair, a broad, sturdy vehicle with two large rear wheels and a smaller one at the front, steered by a set of handlebars. They were perhaps twenty feet from the solicitor's office door when it was thrown open and a large lady, swathed in veils, helped by a pair who were probably a maid and a footman, made her way out.

The progress was far from smooth. The invalid lady needed help over the doorstep and further help to climb into her carriage, but everything her assistants did seemed only to irritate her. She uttered a stream of irritable commands. 'Take my hand, Timpson, my hand. Here man, *here*! Betty! My stick, put it here. *Here*, I say. And the cover, I need the cover. Quickly, Betty. Don't touch that brake, Timpson. Remember what happened last time!'

Once installed and covered in blankets and a fitted waterproof cover, the lady waved her stick around her head and shouted in a voice that showed no sign of weakness, 'Home, Timpson! Home! Push me down the hill first. You know the pavement is too narrow to turn here. Turn me round at the bridge. I will not go on the other side. There are pigeons everywhere on that side!'

The footman let off the brake, and with him pushing the vehicle from behind, the party began to descend the hill at some speed. The wheeled chair occupied the whole width of the pavement. It threatened to drive Miss Hazelton and Vita into the street, which, being one of the main thoroughfares in the city, was crowded with carriages and carts, horse omnibuses and cyclists.

'Stand aside!' The passenger in the chair commanded. She waved her stick at Vita and Miss Hazelton, who looked about to see how they could take cover. 'Stand aside, I say! I am an invalid! Show some consideration, can't you?'

At the last moment, a side passage allowed Vita to pull Miss Hazelton out of the wheeled chariot's way and prevent them both being run over. The occupant of the chair continued down the hill, waving pedestrians this way and that, apparently perfectly willing to knock them about the head with her stick if they threatened to bar her way.

Miss Hazelton was still trembling when Vita helped her into the solicitor's office.

'Ah,' he said, stepping forward to greet them. 'I see you met Lady Longbridge on your way in. I shall send for some tea.'

Vita's imagination had conjured up an image of Mr Waring, the long-trusted solicitor, as a venerable elderly gentleman with a grey beard, but the man who sat behind the mahogany desk was probably only in his thirties. He seemed, Vita thought, remarkably calm and good-humoured for someone who had just had dealings with the formidable stick-waving lady they had just encountered. He ushered Miss Hazelton straight into his office, leaving Vita in the waiting room, which had been left in some disarray.

A grey-haired lady with an apron over a severe black outfit was on her hands and knees, picking up the pieces of what appeared to be a broken vase of flowers. As Vita was wondering how long she would have to wait, and wishing she had thought to bring a book to read, this lady suddenly cried, '*ouch!*' and stopped what she was doing. Vita could see blood begin to flow from a cut on the palm of her hand.

'May I help?' Vita said. 'I have a little first aid training.'

'Oh, that wretched woman!' The solicitor's assistant said. 'Every time she comes here, she leaves a trail of disaster. Last year, she managed to break a window with that stick of hers. A vase of flowers is nothing to her.'

Vita helped the lady to her feet and led her to a chair.

'Can I find some water and a clean cloth somewhere?'

'Out the back, though my office there,' she pointed to a small door. 'There should be everything you need.'

Vita soon returned, examined the cut, cleaned it carefully and bound it. 'It is not too deep. The bleeding should stop if you hold it above your heart for a short time.'

'I should have put the vase out of the way. I usually remember, when I hear the three of them arriving, to put all breakables aside, but she took me by surprise today.'

'I believe you mean Lady Longbridge. I have just narrowly escaped being run over by her on Castle Hill.'

'If you want my opinion, she is a public nuisance. I shouldn't speak this way of one of my son's clients, but she is. People like her believe they own the world and all its population and can treat us like slaves and minions. She comes in here regularly to change her will. A maid of thirty years' service fails to dust something, and she is struck out of the mean little amount she would have been left. Then the following week, a distant cousin writes a charming postcard, and she adds a few hundred to his inheritance. She is both tyrannical and whimsical. It is a perfectly revolting combination.'

The lady was sitting in one of the waiting room chairs, holding her hand above her head. Vita, finding the conversation interesting, took over the job of picking up the shards of broken glass. She found an old newspaper and wrapped them, finishing the job under Mrs Waring's directions, with a dustpan and brush. They had introduced themselves by now.

'And I'll tell you another thing,' Mrs Waring said, looking at her hand to see whether the bleeding had stopped. 'She is very slow to pay her bills. Wealthy people often are, in my experience. Working people respect the needs of those they do business with. The Lady Longbridges of this world care for nobody. Oh dear, you'll have to excuse me, Miss Carew. I am a Yorkshirewoman. We tend to be plain spoken. I have been indiscreet, no doubt.'

'Mr Waring did not seem too disturbed by Lady Longbridge, I noticed,' Vita said.

'My son has the patience of a saint. She comes and goes, creating havoc, and my son is always professional and obliging. He would never say a word against her. I don't know how he does it. Victor's education in the law was very hard won - scholarships and careful economies were what got him through. Years of hardship and study - we are humble people. His father died young, but I always encouraged him. And it all comes to this - having to tolerate the ridiculous fancies of a dreadful old lady like Henrietta Longbridge.' Mrs Waring dropped her arm into her lap. 'Oh dear, I am not usually so indiscreet. I hope you will not repeat this.'

'It is the shock of the injury, I expect,' Vita told her.

. . .

LATER, in the cab on the way home, Miss Hazelton also sang the solicitor's praises. 'I always feel so reassured by a visit to Mr Waring. He is a kind man,' she said, 'and so very knowledgeable.'

'And did he answer your questions about what should be done with Mr Flett's belongings?'

'He said I was within my rights to dispose of them immediately, if I wished. But he also said it might be wisest to pack them and store them for a few months, just in case a relative appeared and wanted to claim something.'

'So you will store them?'

'Yes. I shall tell Agnes to leave the boxes in the roof when she returns.'

'Is she not working today?'

'Her mother is unwell. She sent a note to say she could not come. Poor Agnes has many worries.'

CHAPTER 7

'*I* have enough to do without involving myself any further in this odd young man's death, I suppose,' Vita told herself the next morning. It was the day of the anatomy test paper. She had risen early to revise the anatomy of the hand and wrist and had set the great textbook on the desk.

'*The joints formed between the carpus and four inner metacarpal bones are connected together by dorsal, palmar, and interosseous ligaments. The Dorsal Ligaments, the strongest and most distinct, connect the carpal and metacarpal bones on their dorsal surface.*'

However hard she tried to concentrate on Dr Grey's elegant description, the unsatisfactory matter of Albert Flett kept intruding. Vita set her large, well-thumbed copy of Grey's Anatomy aside. She had bought it second hand, and it bore the marks of several previous owners' concentrated study, but she treasured it nonetheless. Now, however, she went back to her notebook and jotted a few questions.

AF punch to the jaw? Who? Why?

41

Postcard?

Hip flask? Man Georgie saw = H.B. Longbridge?

Hole in roof. Why?

Why did AF write H.B. Longbridge's signature?

Who is H.B. Longbridge?

The final question was answered in the morning newspaper. Lady Henrietta Longbridge's sudden death was still front page news. Today's story included an interview with her nephew, Henry Longbridge, student of Mathematics at Pembroke College, the young man grieving the loss of his only surviving relative.

For his part, the Chief Constable of Cambridge Constabulary was quoted as saying that his force was fully engaged in investigating Lady Longbridge's passing, and that an inquest would soon be opened. He was not at liberty to discuss any further details and wished to discourage speculation.

All this Aunt Louisa read aloud over the breakfast table.

'So Henry is Henrietta's heir?' Vita said. 'And named after his aunt, presumably.'

'It seems likely. The less well-off relations named a child after the rich aunt in hopes of winning favour. It is not very subtle, but it is a common enough practice. And it seems to have worked, in this case. Young Henry stands to come into a very substantial fortune indeed. Not that it is proper to gossip about such matters, of course,' Aunt Louisa smiled.

'Why was he visiting Albert Flett, I wonder?' Vita said.

'Was he visiting Albert Flett?'

'Agnes said a man who called himself Brown visited Albert Flett on several occasions. I think it was Henry Longbridge. The initials HBL were on his hip flask.'

'How do you come to know that?' Louisa put down her table napkin, preparing to leave. 'I have another sitting with the dour organist this morning. The portrait is still not going well.'

'Oh, he dropped it in the street. It's a long story,' Vita said. 'But Longbridge didn't visit on the day Albert died. At least Agnes says she let nobody in.' Vita was speaking her own thoughts aloud. 'Unless he sneaked in at the back door. Would that be possible, I wonder?'

Her aunt turned back at the door, just as the maid came in with a tray to clear breakfast. 'Why don't you ask Tabitha? I'm sure she notices all sorts of details we miss.'

Tabitha looked puzzled at this, and went about her business collecting the plates from the table at first, but when Vita invited her to sit for a minute, she agreed.

'This house is almost exactly the same in its interior pattern as Miss Hazelton's at number 142, Tabitha, wouldn't you say?'

'Yes. It is, Miss, as far as I know,' Tabitha agreed. She had a West Country accent, which reminded Vita of home in Devon.

'So if someone wanted to get up to the attics here without anyone in the house noticing, could they do so, do you think?'

'You mean, if they came in the back door?'

'Would that work best?'

'Yes, Miss. If they was quick and had a light step, they could be up the stairs to the attics like lightning and nobody in the house any the wiser.' Tabitha was blushing slightly. 'If you remember rightly, Miss, I did it myself once or twice in the early days. You heard me in the end, but only after I came in and out a fair few times.'

It was true. Tabitha's attic room was the equivalent of Albert Flett's bedroom, and she had once been in the habit of creeping out at night and early in the morning to visit her little niece.

'Agnes is convinced she would hear if anyone came in.'

'Well, Agnes is wrong, Miss, if you want my opinion,' Tabitha said and with a cheerful shrug, she went back to clearing the breakfast things.

VITA DECIDED against taking her copy of Grey's along with her, and put only her own notes into the basket of her bicycle, feeling gloomily that it was too late now to learn anything she didn't already know. Checking her instructions as she put her coat on, she realised the paper was to be taken at Pembroke College, so she pedalled there across town. It was a grey day, but not too cold, and for once the wind had stayed in the Arctic. It would have been a pleasant ride across Parker's Piece and through the busy streets around the market, if she hadn't been so worried about the tendons of the wrist, of which she could only ever remember four out of five, though irritatingly not always the same four.

At the porter's lodge, the senior porter gave her a cold look at first, not being used to young ladies addressing him purposefully, but softened a little when she explained that she had come for an examination and asked him where it was to be held.

'Well, now,' he said. 'Just let me see.' He peered in an unhurried manner at the large book on the desk, which contained all college appointments and details of every event that day. He ran his finger up and down for a few moments, and then said, 'Ah yes, Anatomy, that would be at ten o'clock.'

'Oh, I thought it was half-past nine,' Vita said.

'From ten o'clock to twelve noon, it says here, Miss. You

are a little early, but you're welcome to sit over there by the fire and wait.' He pointed to a small armchair tucked away alone in the far corner of the ancient lodge building.

There was no choice, so Vita perched in the armchair and tried to focus on her notes while she waited.

Traffic in the porter's lodge was brisk. Students came and went to the pigeonholes along one side, collecting and reading their messages. Packets and parcels were delivered by carters and deliverymen and in between the porters read the newspaper and talked between themselves or joked with the other staff - housekeepers, bedmakers and maids who were reporting for duty and being issued lists of special duties for the day.

One of the younger porters was sorting a pile of letters into the students' pigeonholes. 'Mister Longbridge seems very popular all of a sudden,' he remarked. 'I can hardly fit all his letters in.'

'If you have a look at my newspaper, you might see why,' said the senior man. His two junior colleagues both paused to read their senior colleague's newspaper, which lay on the desk.

'I didn't know he studied Maths. *Mathematics student at Pembroke College*, it says here,' one said.

'He'll need to be good at mathematics to count all that money. He stands to get millions, I heard, now that his old aunt's dead and gone.'

'Blimey,' said the other, looking at the newspaper over his fellow porter's shoulder.

A TAILOR's lad delivered a parcel which had to be signed for, and the porter rang a small bell on his counter summoning a college errand boy. 'Parcel for Mr Willoughby, Hugh, and be quick about it.'

Vita, although she tried to concentrate on the anatomy of the hand, could not help but feel they were discussing Henry Longbridge. It was difficult not to listen.

'He'll give up his studies now, I suppose,' one of the men remarked. 'Who needs mathematics if you are as rich as that?'

'That is a very uneducated attitude,' the senior porter said severely. 'I fear you are correct, all the same. Just between us, young Mr Longbridge is a lot more dedicated to night climbing and the gee-gees than to mathematics. He's retaken the examination at least three times. Gave me a good tip in the summer, though. I won nearly three shillings on Ruby Shamrock in the Gold Cup. Remember that, Jack?'

'I do remember! You weren't sober for two days.'

'Keep your voice down,' the other porter said, nodding towards Vita, who pretended to be absorbed in the ligaments and tendons listed in the notes she was looking at.

'It's supposed to be Longbridge who hung that great spider's web across the great court the year before last. Not just him. Him and the other climbers. D'you see it Jack?'

'That was before I started.'

'A giant spider's web made of ropes. Right across from one side of the court to the other. Nobody saw how it went up. They shinned across it, four or five of them as dawn came up, just like spiders, and then they took the whole thing down. It was gone by six.'

'That sounds like a tall tale to me,' the other said.

'It's true, isn't it, Mr Higgins? Someone even set a camera up and took a photograph.'

'Young fools,' the senior man remarked. 'It's a wonder they don't get themselves killed. You wouldn't catch me shinning around the rooftops and parapets in the middle of the night.'

The two younger porters burst out laughing at this because the man in question was no athlete to judge from his build, and the thought of him scaling the sheer wall of a college building struck them as highly comical.

CHAPTER 8

*V*ita counted three young women and thirty-seven men in the hall as the examination papers were distributed. She knew some of the men and all the other women by sight, but only Mary Mackenzie, another Newton College student by name. Mary was pale and sat at the next desk, twisting her pencil through her fingers. 'It's the viva that I fear most. What about you, Vita?' she said, whispering as they waited.

'Viva? Is there a viva?'

'Yes. Immediately after the paper.'

'I didn't know!' Vita made a face of despair.

'Ten questions face to face with the professor or one of his lecturers.'

'Oh no, no, no! How could I not have known?'

'They tell me it is worse that facing a lion in the gladiator's ring.'

'Oh, come now, Mary. We will not be killed and chewed up, at least.'

'It will amount to the same thing. I am going to fail! I know it!' Mary groaned, clasping her fists to her temples.

'You will not fail, Mary. Take deep breaths and stay calm,' Vita hissed back.

The student at the desk on the other side looked coldly over and frowned at their whispered drama.

'*I am going to fail and be thrown out as well*,' Vita thought. She followed her own advice and took a deep breath. A man in a long academic gown paced the aisles, placing a question paper on each desk. His shoes squeaked on the wooden floor.

'You have ninety minutes,' he announced. 'You will find written at the top of your paper the room and time of your viva examination. Go there as soon as you finish this paper. Wait outside the room until you are called. You may turn over the paper and begin.'

THE TIME PASSED in a blur of anxiety and a jumble of anatomical terms. One minute she seemed to be catching Mary's eye with a sympathetic wink as they turned their question papers over; the next, the man in the noisy shoes was collecting her answers, bundling the papers together and carrying them away.

'What did you think?' Mary said, as they left the hall.

'I can't tell. I knew some of it,' Vita said. 'What about you?'

'I am better on the hand than the wrist. I think a *few* of my answers were correct. I forgot which side the triangular is on. I had to guess.'

They parted outside to find their viva examination rooms. Vita's was up a steep stone staircase. The door had a small wooden bench outside it. The passageway was unheated and seemed to funnel the east wind straight onto her hands and feet. Vita huddled with her hands wrapped around her body and was just wondering whether frostbite of the brain was a genuine medical condition, when the door opened. A young man stepped out and mumbled that she should go in immediately.

'Second door,' he said. 'Don't knock. Just go in.'

On the second door, a beautifully written temporary nameplate read 'Dr Marcus Underhill'. In the delirium of cold and examinations, Vita vaguely thought that she had heard the name before, but couldn't place it. Then she stepped inside, and before her sat the Police Surgeon whose post mortem she had gate crashed.

'Sit down,' he said without looking up from his notes. 'I shall begin with questions about the bones of the wrist.'

Underhill picked a small bone from a box on the desk and placed it in front of her. 'Name this, please.'

It was a complicated little bone about half an inch across, with indents and craters on all sides. Vita looked at it for a moment and felt the silence of the college room bear down upon her as if the air had thickened. Every name she had ever learnt flew from her head and left it blank. *Deep breaths.*

Underhill leaned back in his chair and looked out of the window.

'May I touch it?' Vita asked, hoping to win herself a little more time.

'Of course,' he said with a bored sigh. He did not look round.

The sensation of turning the small bone over in her fingers brought some of the names back. *Carpus. Metacarpus. Phalange.* The drawing of the skeletal hand from Gray's textbook began, piece by piece, to assemble itself in her memory. 'It is a capitate, I believe,' she said.

'Left or right?' Underhill asked, still preoccupied with something outside the window.

'Left, I think.'

'You *think*?'

'Well, if the lunate is at the top and the navicular is to the right, that would make it the left capitate. Yes, the left.' She sounded definite enough for Underhill to turn and look at her over his spectacles.

'Well, you seem to know more than the previous candidate, at least,' he said, without enthusiasm. 'Articulations?'

'Of the capitate?'

'Yes. Can you list the articulations of the capitate - the bones it is in contact with?'

Vita swallowed. The little wrist bone she still held came from right in the centre, surrounded by the tight cluster of irregular shapes that made up the complex articulation of the wrist - the most mobile and complicated joint in the whole body. *Breathe.* She had spent hours poring over the description. By closing her eyes, she could see the page of the book in her mind's eye, the paragraph under the illustrated skeletal hand which pointed down towards it.

'Would you mind answering, Miss Carew? Another candidate is waiting.'

'Seven,' Vita said. 'It articulates with seven bones.'

'Thank you. I asked the names. Name them, if you please.'

'Three metacarpals.'

'Which ones?'

'The middle ones.'

'That is not acceptable as an answer. We do not say *the middle ones.*'

'The second, third and fourth.'

'That is better. What else?'

'Well, I mentioned the navicular and the lunate before.'

'Yes. That brings us to five out of the seven.' Underhill

began to tap his foot under the table. Vita could feel it vibrate with his impatience. She frowned, and stared at the small bone in her hand, touching the indentations where it would fit among the other bones like the complicated jigsaw puzzle it was. 'Then there is the multangular on this side,' she said.

'Which side?'

'The right?'

'What do we call it in anatomy instead of calling it *the right*?'

'The radial, sorry.'

Underhill sighed again, and this time shook his head too, briefly. 'Oh, do come on, Miss Carew. I can't wait all day.'

'The hamate!' Vita said. 'The hamate on the ulnar side.'

'Now list them again,' he said.

Vita placed the little bone back on the desk and sat up straight. 'Navicular, lunate, second, third and fourth metacarpals, lesser multangular and hamate.'

'Good. That will be all.'

'All?'

'That is the end of your viva. You may leave.'

Having lost all sense of time, Vita could only pick up her bag and bolt.

'I imagine you will want to observe the post mortem,' Underhill remarked as she reached the door. He was looking down at his notes, writing. 'I refer to my examination of the unfortunate Lady Longbridge.'

Vita turned in surprise. 'Yes. I would very much like to observe.'

'Monday morning at eight,' he said. 'Don't be late. And don't ask too many questions. I'd like to be finished in time for lunch.'

. . .

THE MISERABLE-LOOKING young man waiting on the bench in the cold passageway outside looked anxiously up. 'You look cheerful,' he said. 'I heard Underhill is a hard examiner. What did he ask?'

'The articulations of the capitate,' Vita said, 'among other things.'

The student let out a groan and threw his head back in a gesture of utter despair.

CHAPTER 9

The gymnasium was noisy. A dozen boys in white sportsman's clothing were performing rhythmic calisthenic exercises under her brother's leadership. Edward stood on a podium at the front, demonstrating the movements and calling instructions.

'And *lift*. The right hand should be over the shoulder. We aim for a stretch of the whole right side of the body. A little more. Good, and the other side… Do not hold your breath. Your breathing should be steady and even.'

Vita tiptoed along the wall into the back office, where her brother's employer, Aloysius Derbyshire, an elegant figure in his white fencing clothes, was practising moves with his sword. Derbyshire was a fencing instructor of national repute. Cups and medallions lined the shelves behind the desk.

'Miss Carew,' he said, without interrupting his practice, 'what can we do for you?'

'You would encounter many of the more sporting young men of the university, I suppose, Mr Derbyshire, in your occupation,' Vita said.

Holding his epée horizontal, he bent his front knee and

plunged forward as if spearing an opponent's heart. 'I would, naturally,' he agreed.

'Have you heard of night climbers?'

'Of course.' Derbyshire leapt back to a formal standing position, his blade upright in front of his face. 'They are the chaps who scale the peaks of the ancient buildings around here and leave wigs or dunce's hats on the noble statuary.'

'What sort of person would do this, Mr Derbyshire, in your opinion?'

'A foolish sort. It is dangerous. Although I must admit there is a certain dash to inspiring awe anonymously.'

'They act anonymously?'

'Oh yes.' Derbyshire swished his thin sword, slicing the air in a figure of eight on either side of his body. Vita was glad she had stayed on the other side of the room. 'They are notoriously secretive. Nobody ever admits to being a night climber.'

Vita thought about this for a moment. Henry Longbridge was certainly not very good at keeping his night climbing secret, if the porters all seemed to know about it.

'Of course, they are also as vain as peacocks - most young men are - so they usually find a way of letting it be known. It is said to be most impressive to the ladies, and so on. But what is your interest in night climbing, Miss Carew? Are you in pursuit of some wrong-doer?'

'Certainly not,' Vita replied, annoyed that Derbyshire had guessed so quickly. 'How is Edward lately?'

'She changes the subject, I see. I must be on to something.' the sportsman was looking pleased with himself.

'I am trying to find out as much as possible about a student called Henry Longbridge...'

'Oh yes, we know Henry Longbridge. He was a regular

here at the gymnasium until a few weeks ago, and then no sign of him, and an unpaid bill.'

'Really? What sort of man is he?'

'The sort who does not settle his bills. Why do you ask?'

'He seems to have been a friend or business contact of our neighbour's lodger who has been found dead.'

'I say, Miss Carew, you are not involving yourself in something of that sort, surely? Does your aunt know? Are university studies not enough to keep your mind thoroughly occupied?'

Vita sighed. 'I certainly do have far too much to do, but there's something odd, and all I can tell is that Longbridge seems to be connected with it.'

'And the police?'

'They are preoccupied with the death of Longbridge's aunt.'

'Ah yes, I read about that.' Derbyshire put his sword into its rack on the wall. 'I have a private client in five minutes,' he said, 'but in answer to your question, Longbridge is a well-connected young fellow, but we found him unpleasant. Inclined to be rude and impatient. Limited staying power. He trained in weight lifting and on the wall bars, and made some progress, but hadn't the persistence. He has a naturally good physique, but I'd guess he drinks too much. He hasn't the character for serious physical training. Ah, here is my client arriving.'

As Derbyshire left, Vita's brother Edward came in and threw himself into the office's only chair. 'What brings you here, Sis?'

'I fear I have just botched an anatomy test paper,' Vita said.

'Which one?'

'The hand and wrist.'

'Shame. Well, the hand and wrist *are* complicated.'

'But you must have remembered them.'

'Perhaps once. I couldn't tell you much about them now.'

'Will you return to medicine, Edward?'

'I don't know. I know our father longs for me to do so, but I like it well enough here in the gym for now. I have a few more months to decide.'

'Did you meet Henry Longbridge when he came here? Derbyshire said he was a client.'

'Yes. A difficult client. Always knew best and argued with his instructors - me, in particular. Why?'

'Oh, I was just curious. His name keeps coming up.'

'Ah, that is my next client - Miss Robertson, for Oriental Self-defence.'

'You teach Oriental Self-defence to ladies?'

'Indeed yes. I have studied the works of Emiliano Chan, the great expert from New York.'

'How interesting! And is Miss Robertson an apt student?'

'She certainly is. Any villain who grapples with Miss Robertson will rue the day. She represents her college in three different sports, is a skilled horsewoman and a trained member of her college's student fire brigade. Today we practise methods of escaping a strangle hold.'

'I may ask you to show that to me sometime, Edward. It sounds most interesting.'

A young woman walked by the office door in her hat and coat, nodding a brief greeting to Edward as she passed.

Vita couldn't help noticing the large smile Miss Robertson's minimal greeting brought to her brother's face.

THE CART BELONGING to the firm of Petit and Sons, General Builders, was a familiar presence in Eden Street. The Petits did all the local house repairs. Mr Petit's patient chestnut mare stood outside Miss Hazelton's house and twitched her ears as Vita cycled up. Mr Petit senior was holding a very long ladder against the side of the house, and one of his sons - he had several, all black-haired, strong and great assets to the business - was at the top, inspecting the hole in the roof.

'How many slates missing, Bob?' Mr Petit shouted.

'Fourteen,' the distant voice of his son called down from the top of the ladder.

A different dark-haired head stuck itself through the hole in the roof. Another Petit lad was clearly inspecting from the inside. It called something, but it couldn't be heard.

'What d'he say?' Mr Petit senior yelled.

'There are twelve inside,' shouted the son at the top of the ladder, relaying what his brother in the roof space had said.

'How many broken?'

The head poking out of the roof retracted for a moment or two and then reappeared. It communicated with the man at the top of the ladder, who shouted, 'None, Pa. All in one piece.'

'What none broken?' Petit senior shouted.

'None!' the two high-up Petits replied. 'Only the nails twisted.'

'Well, I never!' Mr Petit declared, as Vita passed him. 'I never seen that before. Fourteen tiles off and only two broken that fell to the ground. The others fell inwards.'

He said this to nobody in particular.

'Was it the wind?' Vita asked. She was not the only passer-by to have paused to watch the Petits at work. They were quite used to an audience.

'Must've been. It didn't have anyone else's tiles off that night, though.'

There was a brief pause as Mr Petit scratched his head and the lad up the ladder climbed down. Vita parked her bicycle in the back garden. She was about to go into her aunt's back door when the son who had been in Miss Hazelton's attic roof came round the side of the house and rejoined his father.

'What happened up there then?' said Mr Petit.

'That don't look like no wind damage to me, Pa. Them tiles was pulled off, I should say.'

His father shrugged. He did not have much time for speculation. He had a business to run. 'Should be a nice quick job for us, anyway.'

Vita heard this as she opened the back door. She laid her anatomy notes on her desk, then ran back downstairs to ask Mr Petit a final question.

CHAPTER 10

That Saturday was a working day for both Vita and her aunt, but only half an hour into her books, with the familiar smell of turpentine drifting up the stairs from her aunt's studio, Vita was called by Tabitha to speak to Constable Williamson.

'I'm sent to take your statement, Miss Carew. About what you saw when you found Albert Flett.'

In the sitting room, Vita went over the events of that afternoon, and the constable wrote them. His handwriting was tidy and clear, she noted, the sort of handwriting a schoolteacher would feel proud of in a favourite pupil.

'And did Miss Hazelton's maid say anything to you about letting a visitor in?' he asked.

'She said Mr Flett did sometimes have visitors, but that he had not received a visit from anyone that day. You asked her whether she was sure she would hear someone if they entered through the back door. She was quite certain she would hear them, even if she had been in the basement kitchen.'

'She has remembered a caller now,' Constable

Williamson said, looking up. 'She remembers opening the door to a man called Brown. A regular caller, apparently.'

Vita looked at the constable in surprise. 'How strange that she forgot. But I suppose it was all very upsetting. Did she describe this Mr Brown?'

Williamson looked earnestly at Vita. 'A tall gentleman,' she said. And ill-mannered. Rude to her on the doorstep. Impatient.'

Vita decided to venture a theory. 'A man of that description dropped a hip flask on the night that Albert Flett died. He dropped it in Fitzroy Street and someone picked it up - the pawnshop owner, Mr Bradley - who put it in the window so that it could be reclaimed.'

'Norman Bradley!' the constable repeated. 'I know Bradley well enough. He's had one or two brushes with the law himself.'

'Well, he restored the hip flask to its owner. It had the initials HBL on it, and the gentleman - a tall man and curt in his manner - said his name was Henry Longbridge. The point is,' Vita went on, 'that the caller who had identified himself to Agnes as Mr Brown on several occasions, might really be Henry Longbridge.'

Williamson looked unconvinced. 'Agnes Venner was not very clear about anything when I spoke to her. She makes a poor witness. She contradicted herself and was uncertain of times and practically all other details. She was upset and nervous. She couldn't think straight.'

'Well, that is understandable enough. She had a shock,' Vita said, 'although, on the whole, Agnes has always seemed very level-headed to me.'

'She was so fretful she could barely put a sentence together.'

'Did she see anyone leave the house that afternoon?' Vita asked.

'No, but as I said, she was not very ordered in her account of the events. To be honest, Miss, she was so tearful, it was hard to get much sense out of her.'

'Henry Longbridge is a night climber,' Vita said. 'I found that out at his college.'

'One of those foolish young jack-an-apes who risk their neck climbing college buildings for a joke?' Williamson said, looking up from his notes. 'They haven't the sense they were born with, if you ask me.'

'Yes. The thing is, I found a hole in the roof when I was helping Agnes put Albert Flett's belongings into the roof space.'

'I saw the workmen repairing it,' the police officer said. 'The roof was in bad repair, I suppose. Or damaged in the storm. We've had bad weather.'

'But the slates fell inwards and someone piled them up *inside* the roof. The builders said that only two fell off the roof and broke. The others could have been removed from the inside.'

Constable Williamson looked at Vita, puzzled.

'I couldn't make sense of it either,' Vita went on. 'Apart from the builder, I am the only one who has been in the roof next door - Agnes can't get in there because of her bad back - I saw the hole and the slates, but I didn't make anything of it until I saw the Petits at work. They said the nails that hold the slates on had been twisted and wrenched. I think someone hid in the roof space and made their way out through the roof by pulling off the slates.'

'Is that possible? To poke a hole in a roof from the inside?' Williamson did not seem to think it likely.

'The roof, as you said, was not in the best repair. I could

see daylight in several places. There was no lining beneath the slates. Someone fairly strong - which Longbridge is - could push out a couple of slates, perhaps using their feet, and then reach through the hole and prize off the dozen or so more that would need to be moved to make a hole big enough to climb out of. It might take time, but he was in no hurry.'

Williamson shook his head. 'That's three storeys up. It's a terrible long drop.'

'There's a drainpipe. I checked. I asked Mr Petit if it would be strong enough. He said it was well fixed to the wall and strong enough to bear a man's weight. The hole was right on the corner of the roof. I think Longbridge went out right over the drainpipe. He's a good climber. He could easily shin down and get away.'

'Why not just creep down the stairs?'

'Because people might be there. He would have over-heard us talking. He would have known I was there first, then you arrived, and Inspector Llewellyn came a little later. There had been a lot of comings and goings. For all he knew, a constable might have been left to stand guard.'

'You think he hid there in the roof and listened? Waited there until it was night?'

'It is certainly possible. And he would have heard us saying that it looked like an unlucky accident. None of us knew about the roof space. You and I looked around the two rooms, but we didn't search any further. We had no reason to. But that was before the post mortem confirmed the bruise on Albert Flett's chin.'

'Inspector Llewellyn is still inclined to think it was an accident.'

'Even now that Lady Henrietta has died so suspiciously?'

Williamson held up his hands. 'Wait a minute! There is a *possible* connection to Henry Longbridge, but so far only that he *might* have visited Flett once or twice and *might* have come on the day he died, but Agnes Venner can't even be certain of that.'

'But if she did see him, and he did climb out of the roof and escape? The important thing is that if Henry Longbridge killed Albert Flett, why shouldn't he have killed his aunt as well?' Vita said. She was a little breathless by now.

Williamson stared at her wide-eyed for a moment and then drew himself up. 'You have jumped an awful long way to that conclusion, if I may say so, Miss Carew.'

'I know,' Vita said. 'There are a few details missing, as yet, but surely it would be worth your while to look into the two deaths as if they were connected?'

'I'm not sure what the Inspector will have to say about that.'

'But you will put it to him? I would do so myself, but he is not inclined to listen to me for one reason or another.'

'Once I have added to my notes back at the station, I shall consider it,' Williamson said with dignity.

Tabitha appeared at the door.

'Excuse me, Miss. Your aunt wondered if you would like some tea brought up.'

'No, thank you Tabitha, we have finished here now. But do by all means offer the constable a cup of tea in the kitchen,' Vita said.

This arrangement appeared to suit both the maid and Constable Williamson.

CHAPTER 11

'I have had to send Agnes home, I'm afraid. She is not herself since poor Albert died. It is most kind of you to call, Vita.'

Miss Hazelton had answered her own front door, and now ushered Vita into her sitting room, as crowded with lace and paintings of flowers as ever. In every direction she looked, Vita saw another ornamental stuffed bird, plant or embroidered screen. The old lady sat on a tiny armchair draped with a flowery shawl and invited Vita to take a button-backed fireside chair. This turned out to be so low that Vita found her legs awkwardly folded as she looked up at her hostess.

'I hope you are well yourself, Miss Hazelton,' she said. 'It has been distressing.'

'Yes, indeed,' Miss Hazelton said, but she appeared distracted. 'It was kind of you to go to all the way Bainbridge's and let them know.' She looked away and her fingers played with the long fringe of the shawl. 'Vita, may I speak to you in confidence?'

'Is something worrying you?' Vita asked.

'It may be nothing, Dear, but... I don't wish to cause

anyone any trouble. Or to make matters worse than they already are.'

'No, naturally,' Vita tried to sound encouraging.

'It is only that I have had doubts about Albert for some time. I should perhaps have mentioned this to Inspector Llewellyn when he was here, but he was so brisk and businesslike, you know, so very busy and formal. And it may amount to nothing. If I mention one or two small matters to you, would you perhaps listen and help me to decide whether I should tell the police officers, Dear?'

'Of course,' Vita said.

Miss Hazelton smiled at her guest. 'You are so kind. I so admire the modern sort of young woman, Vita. You have marvellously broad horizons; you are fearless! I was brought up to fear my own shadow. Ladies swooned at the sight of a mouse in my youth; we feared the heat, the cold, draughts, chills - we feared everything! We took to our beds for weeks with the slightest ailment. We were wrapped in cotton wool from our earliest days. I had a cousin who was carried everywhere in a chair as a girl because her heart was supposed to be weak, but she is still alive now, at nearly ninety years old. And look at me. My own health was considered delicate, I was kept in, dosed with medicines, discouraged from all exertion, and here I am, eighty-four years old. I look back and think my life has been long, but it has also been shamefully unadventurous. In short it might have been a richer life, if I had ignored all advice and exerted myself a great deal more!'

'What would you have liked to do?' Vita asked.

Miss Hazelton's eyes lit up. 'I should have been a mountaineer! Or at the very least a great walker. I see them nowadays in the newspapers - young women who have scaled the highest peaks here and even in Switzerland. Imagine it, Vita! Clambering over rocks and snow-covered glaciers, hauling oneself up, hand over hand, reaching the summit and looking out over the clouds, with the whole wide landscape spread out below!'

'Have you ever climbed at all?' Vita asked.

'Oh no, I have always lived here in the flattest part of the country! I once went to the Lake District and walked a little there, and once or twice to the Highlands of Scotland. We saw walkers, and the men went on shooting parties, but we ladies always stayed inside. We saw mountain peaks through binoculars or in the distance as we walked the gardens. Climbing was out of the question for us.'

The old lady sighed, but then smiled at Vita. 'So, you see, Vita, I love to think of hearty young women being able to climb mountains, or study science or travel to far-off countries. Your exciting lives will make up for all the restrictions my sisters and I endured! But all this is only wasting your time. I asked you here because I want to tell you about Albert. Now, Vita, I don't want you to be too shocked, but I have known for some time that Albert was not always telling me the truth about his life.'

Vita looked at the old lady, waiting.

'He ate dinner with me at least twice a week. It was always the arrangement I had with my lodgers. With many of them it was, frankly, a trial. They were often very poor company, but Albert was different. Albert was a most entertaining guest. His stories about Bainbridge's and the people he worked with were delightful. He filled my Tuesday and Sunday evenings with colourful stories. There was always something going on - a scandal, a rivalry, a comical incident. I came to know the names, the different characters, their quirks and eccentricities. We laughed and laughed together. His stories painted a picture of a glamorous and colourful world. I was utterly charmed. *But*,' Miss Hazelton glanced down at her hands briefly, then back up and looked Vita in the eye. 'I knew very little of it was true.'

Vita looked at the old lady in astonishment. 'You did not believe his stories? But why not? What made you doubt him?'

Miss Hazelton smiled and shrugged. 'My memory for the details was better than Albert's, I suppose. He often contradicted himself. He 'improved' the stories every time we ate together. As time went on, I decided not to concern myself. Listening to Albert was like hearing the next chapter of a very entertaining novel, or waiting for the next episode of a magazine story. I understood that much of it was untrue, but I thoroughly enjoyed it, nonetheless. I was entertained. I was perfectly content with the arrangement. What did it matter if Albert told me tales? They were marvellously enjoyable tales!'

Miss Hazelton looked into the distance, still smiling, for a moment, but then her expression changed and she looked back at Vita. 'But then I also began to wonder what else he was fabricating. If he invented his life at Bainbridge's, what else had he made up? Was he employed there at all? Was Albert Flett really his name? Was he really an orphan? All these things did cross my mind. I should have taken action, I suppose, but Albert was such pleasant company.'

Something occurred to Vita. 'He did not ask you for money, did he?'

'Money? Oh, no. Never.' The old lady looked shocked. 'In all honesty, my dear, if he had, I should probably have given it to him, not that I have much to spare. No, he never asked for money, but I suppose he did ask *something* in return for his company.'

Vita waited again, wondering what the old lady would say next.

'Without asking in so many words, I suppose he did hope for a certain discretion. He hoped I would not ask too many questions, and I was happy to oblige. People came and went occasionally from his rooms, some of them used the back door. As long as matters stayed within the limits of reasonable behaviour - not too much noise; no callers after seven in the evening - which they always did, I was happy to leave Albert to live his own life. He appeared very hard-working. He kept to a weekly routine. If his movements did not exactly tally with what he told me over one of our dinners, I felt no need to inquire any further. Should I have mentioned this to Inspector Llewellyn, Vita?'

'There isn't much to tell, is there?' Vita said. 'Only that you had a feeling that your lodger was not always truthful.' She shifted on the low chair, trying to move her legs into a comfortable position, but it was difficult. 'Miss Hazelton, did you ever wonder whether Albert was involved in any criminal activity?'

'I have led a sheltered life, Vita. No doubt I appear unworldly and gullible to many, but I am not foolish. It did occur to me that Albert and his visitors might be involved in something underhand, but since it did not involve unpleasantness of any sort in my house - not, that is, until earlier this week - I asked no questions. I regret that bitterly now. I might have been able to help the dear boy. I feel I have let him down. He was a friendly companion to me, and I did not do my duty.'

'You must not hold yourself responsible, Miss Hazelton. There seem to be forces at work here that nobody understands as yet.'

Miss Hazelton nodded, then leaned forward and spoke urgently to Vita. 'My dear, I feel so helpless. If there is anything you can do - you who are so energetic and resourceful - I would be endlessly grateful. You have a talent, your Aunt tells me, for finding explanations. I beg you, Vita, if there is any way you can help to explain what happened to poor Albert, please do pursue the matter. Root around; ask questions; press on with your inquiries, even if the police officers have lost interest, there may be answers that you can find.'

This was not the end to the conversation that Vita had expected. 'Well, of course. I will do whatever I can,' she began to say, 'but Miss Hazelton, I might uncover things that reflect badly on Albert Flett, or on others.'

'I seek the truth, Vita. I am perfectly strong enough to cope with unpleasantness or difficulty, as long as I can be satisfied that someone has taken the trouble to find the true explanation for the death of that unfortunate young man. If it really was an accident, I shall have to accept it, but I cannot help but have my doubts.'

'Very good,' Vita said, 'in that case, I should like to begin by looking again at the attic rooms. And I only hope that I can justify the faith you put in me.'

CHAPTER 12

*L*ouisa needed little encouragement to visit Bainbridge's, so Vita and her aunt both took the train to London the next morning. As they stepped from the grand revolving doors, Louisa said, 'Find me in Gloves or Millinery, Dear, when you're ready,' and headed for her favourite departments.

The great store was a palace of luxuries, impressive even to Vita, who generally preferred libraries to shops. The perfumery hall alone seemed the size of a cathedral. Bewilderingly scented and sparkling, it was lit by vast chandeliers. Staff behind their brass-railed counters were glamorous in stylish uniforms. Vita made her way through, assailed on every side by clouds of perfume, and eventually found the quiet corner where a young woman sat at a desk near the stairs giving directions. She seemed surprised when Vita asked for the administrative offices, but directed her towards a discreet door right at the back of the store. There, Vita left the public part of the shop and stepped behind the scenes, a very different place, with narrow corridors, storerooms and staff in Bainbridge's royal blue livery hurrying about, busy, but off-stage and full of jokes and gossip. A passing doorman, a grand figure in his gold braided uniform, offered to guide her to the personnel department, and after several corridors and sets of stairs, showed Vita into an office where an elegant middle-aged clerk sat at a desk.

'Yes?' said this lady, as Vita looked into the room.

'I was hoping to speak to someone about a member of staff who worked here at Bainbridge's,' Vita said.

'Certainly. Come in and take a seat.' The brisk lady behind the desk closed the ledger she was writing in and looked expectantly at her visitor. 'And the employee's name?'

'Albert Flett.'

'Flett? That rings no bells with me. Ruby!' She called the name past Vita's shoulder towards a side office. 'Have we an Albert Flett on the books?'

'He was probably in the art department. He was a graphic artist,' Vita added.

'That would be Advertising, then. Is there an Albert Flett in Advertising, Ruby?'

There was a brief pause, as if a list were being consulted. 'None I can see, Miss Parker. Is that F-L-E-double T?' the voice called from behind the glazed door panel.

Miss Parker looked at Vita, who nodded.

'Yes. F-L-E-double T.'

'Nobody of that name, Miss Parker,' called the invisible assistant from the next room.

'He designed posters. He was here twice a week. On a Tuesday and a Friday,' Vita said, adding all she knew about Albert Flett's working life.

'Posters? That might be on the display side, I suppose. Try under Display, Ruby.'

'No, nothing under Display either,' the distant voice replied, after a brief pause.

'May I ask why you are looking for Mr Flett?' Miss Parker enquired.

'I came to inform his employer that Mr Flett has died,' Vita said.

'I see,' said Miss Parker.

'I am a friend of his landlady. He told her he worked here.'

'Well, I have been here for twenty-three years, and I have never seen the name Albert Flett on any staff list, I'm afraid,' said Miss Parker.

'Freelance!' The call came from Ruby. 'His name's on a list of freelance graphic artists, Miss Parker. We paid him last three years ago for a poster advertising hot chocolate.' The young assistant now appeared in the doorway and brought a single document in, placing it with an air of triumph before the senior lady. Miss Parker adjusted her small spectacles and examined the paper.

'We paid him last in October 1902. It looks as if that was a one-off commission for Mr Ridley in Christmas Displays.'

'So he did not come here regularly? Not even as a free-lancer?' Vita asked.

'No, he would be on the records if we paid him regularly.'

Vita was too confused to speak.

'Please accept our condolences,' Miss Parker added, as an afterthought.

'You're sure he did not work here?' Vita asked again, as she stood to leave.

'Certain. We run a tight ship here at Bainbridge's Personnel, don't we, Ruby?'

'Yes, Miss Parker,' her assistant confirmed, as she retreated behind the frosted glass door.

. . .

'Ah, Vita! Please, Dear, take me away from this place. I am in danger of spending Mr Pottendale's fee before the portrait is finished, and that never ends well. Have you seen these gloves? Look at that scarlet pair with the buttons! Look at the cerise! Quite beautiful! But the price! I must leave immediately. But then again, I do genuinely have need of a new pair. And these fur linings!'

Vita took her aunt's elbow and gently walked her away from the temptations of the glove counter. But Bainbridge's was cunningly designed so that a shopper planning to escape had still to pass a great many appealing displays before she reached the door. There were long pauses at millinery: 'I'll just glance at the Spring fashions, Dear, just for inspiration. Hat shops in Cambridge can be very provincial'; Upholstery and Curtains: 'The dining room really does need something brighter at the windows, don't you think?'; and Art Materials: 'Goodness, that is a shocking price for watercolour paper!' before they could escape.

'So he never really worked there at all?' Aunt Louisa asked once they were settled in the train on the way home.

'Perhaps he was at a different department store. There are several on Oxford Street,' Vita said.

'It was always Bainbridge's that he mentioned to Miss Hazelton, I believe.'

'Yes, that's what she told me, too.' Vita looked out at the dappled grey of the sky as they left the tunnels outside King's Cross Station.

'He was not telling the truth, then?'

'Apparently not. He seems to have made up stories about his life at Bainbridge's after having completed a single piece of work for them.'

'Well, it entertained Miss Hazelton, I suppose,' said Aunt Louisa.

'Should I tell her he was inventing it all?'

'Perhaps not. She was fond of him. You could just say you have informed them of his death and leave it at that. It might be kinder.'

'Yes,' Vita said, 'the police may not be so tactful, though.'

'I suppose not,' her aunt agreed, 'if they even ask any questions. They appear to be satisfied that Albert Flett's death was an unfortunate accident.'

'But someone had punched him on the jaw! I saw the bruise. The post mortem confirmed it.' A lady on the other side of the carriage looked across in some alarm. Vita lowered her voice. 'It seems very suspicious. How could they not pursue that?'

'Perhaps they have other things on their plate, dear,' said her aunt, and began looking through the half dozen packages she had carried away from Bainbridge's, despite not being there for long.

CAMBRIDGE STATION, when they arrived, was so thronged that even climbing out of the train was not easy. There seemed to be some sort of hub-hub near the newspaper seller's shop. People were crowding round.

'Something in the newspapers must be drawing the crowds. I wonder what it could be?' Louisa wondered.

'Shall I join the queue?' Vita offered.

'Dear me, no,' said her aunt, 'that scrummage is no place for a young woman. I'll send a porter.'

A sixpence in the hand of the nearest porter and a copy of the Cambridge News was soon theirs. The headline drawing everyone's attention was on the front page: ***Shocking Death of Prominent Cambridge Resident. Foul Play Suspected.*** *Cambridge Constabulary this morning announced the death* *of Lady Henrietta Longbridge, long-time resident of the city and benefactrice of numerous local charities. A well-known figure in the city, Lady Longbridge, was found dead in suspicious circumstances at her home in Chesterton Road.*

'I saw her only yesterday. She was alive and well and frightening pedestrians on Castle Hill,' Vita remarked.

'Well, the pedestrians of Cambridge need fear her stick no longer,' said her aunt. 'May she rest in peace. She was a charitable woman in her way. And her eccentricities enlivened the city for many years, even if she did terrify the populace wherever she went in her bath chair. The Longbridge family has been rather prominent in our lives recently, Vita, dear. I imagine that is something you will be looking into.'

They were outside the station by now, and hurrying towards Eden Street. An icy rain was thickening into sleet.

'I have an anatomy examination to prepare for,' Vita said, falling into step beside her aunt. 'I have absolutely no time for anything else.'

Her aunt only raised one eyebrow at that.

CHAPTER 13

*N*ot knowing where to start in the attic room, Vita placed Albert Flett's hard little desk chair in the middle of the sitting room and sat on it to survey the room in detail. She did not know what she was looking for. Only that there might be something that would help to explain what happened there. What was noticeable? It was cold, that was one thing, but then the fire had not been lit for several days. The curtains and furniture were the same. The hearth rug was different. Agnes had replaced the bloodstained one.

The corner of the deadly black marble mantel shelf was now perfectly clean, but as hard and sharp as ever. Vita went on her hands and knees and peered at the iron fender rail's castellated pattern. That, too, seemed easily hard enough to break a skull or bruise a chin.

Look hard enough and murderous hazards appear everywhere, Vita thought, *every door handle and coat hook becomes a deadly danger.*

She remembered the notebooks she and Agnes had found. So many pages had been removed. How would Flett have disposed of them? By burning them in the fireplace? Vita leaned forward and peered into the grate. A few coals remained with soft grey ash beneath them and here and there she thought she could see charred and twisted ends of paper. She eased several of these out, but they crumbled or revealed nothing she could read.

As she dusted the soot from her fingers and sat back on her heels, she felt a very slight movement in the floorboards under the rug. She moved and lifted it aside. Two of the boards just in front of the fireplace had been very tidily cut. They formed a small panel, which Vita prized open to uncover a gap beneath the flooring. Feeling inside, she found only chilly air. It was empty.

Vita examined the pinewood floorboard panel she had lifted aside. Workmen often sawed floorboards in order to make repairs. She had seen the rough and ragged ends this left. Since they were often concealed under furniture or rugs, they were rarely perfectly repaired. But these boards had been meticulously re-sealed and the raw edges plugged with a brown coloured sawdust paste all the way round. This was now crumbled where the boards had been prized open. She could smell the pinewood sawdust. It seemed to be a carefully constructed hiding place, but whatever it had hidden was no longer there.

She remembered Agnes, so eager to clean the rug. Agnes who was upset and behaving oddly, and who had been sent home. She also remembered, as she replaced the floorboards and pulled the rug back over to cover the little place of concealment, that the pawnbroker had said he had something for Agnes. And Vita had not thought to ask any more about it.

She sat on the chair in the middle of the room again, pausing to polish her glasses, which had become clouded with dust and ash. The pawnbroker was unlikely to answer any questions, but he clearly knew Agnes. That would suggest - what? That she used his services? That she was, in other words, regularly in need of ready money?

'Whatever went on in this little room?' she asked aloud. The desk, the rug and the fireplace offered no reply. A church clock struck twelve in the distance. Vita left the attic to keep its secrets and went to ask Miss Hazelton for Agnes's address. She would call on her in the morning.

OVER DINNER THAT EVENING, Aunt Louisa asked about the anatomy examination.

'I seriously fear I may not have answered enough questions correctly. I so wish, Aunt, that I had been able to begin studying science a little earlier. Many of the other students - nearly all the young men, I mean - have many years of scientific study already under their belts.'

'Not many studied anatomy, though, surely?' her aunt said. 'Anatomy is not part of a usual school curriculum. I certainly don't remember my brothers mentioning it at their schools.'

'No, not anatomy, but most of them would have some familiarity with biology and physics. It gives them a strong foundation. A head start, you might say. The young women, who have not had even the slightest exposure to scientific study are at a thorough disadvantage.'

'Perhaps you would prefer a less demanding subject?'

'No, Aunt. I did not mean that.'

'Dancing or perhaps gymnastics might appeal more? Or watercolour landscapes?'

'You are mocking me, Aunt.'

'Or embroidery,' Louisa was beginning to enjoy herself. 'You might take up the violin. The harpsichord is a delightful instrument as well. Many young ladies enjoy the harpsichord.'

'Oh, Aunt! You know I haven't a musical bone in my body - and as for embroidery!'

'I'm sorry, Vita, but I couldn't resist! You were feeling sorry for yourself, and you needed a little reminder of the alternatives life has to offer a young woman of your age.'

'Miss Hazelton told me that she wished she could have been a mountaineer when I saw her this afternoon.'

Louisa laughed. 'I find it a little difficult to imagine Miss Hazelton up a mountain roped and booted, but I was reading only yesterday about some women alpinists. They tackle the most extraordinary peaks nowadays, you know.'

'Her lodger had been lying to her about working at Bainbridge's. Miss Hazelton even suspected as much, but chose not to challenge him. She liked his company and his stories too much.'

'She was perhaps a little lonely. The truth is not always so very important, as you grow older.'

Vita looked in surprise at her Aunt, but Louisa was fully engaged with buttering a bread roll. 'Have you made good progress with the portrait today, Aunt?'

'As a matter of fact, I have. I have finally found a way of awakening Mr Pottendale from his waxwork-like passivity. It was not easy, but after thorough research, I have at last succeeded. I could hardly stop him from talking this morning. He was livelier than I have ever seen him before.'

'And how did you achieve this small miracle?'

'By mentioning moles!'

'Moles? You mean the little black animals that live in burrows?'

'Exactly! It turns out that Mr Pottendale is an extremely

enthusiastic gardener. He is Chair of his college's Garden Committee - an office of the highest importance, apparently.

And moles are the bane of his existence. Since he took up his post, they have begun to dig their little tunnels all over the sacred centuries-old lawns. The damage to the turf is dreadful - the damage to the Chair of the Garden Committee's reputation is even worse! It is his responsibility to rid the college of the dreaded pest, but everything he and the groundsmen have tried has failed. He is absolutely at his wits' end. The mere mention of moles brought the colour rushing into his cheeks. His eyes shone with rage. It was a marvellous improvement on his usual grey indifference!'

Vita laughed. 'But how did you stumble across moles as a topic in the first place?'

'Oh, I can assure you that was no accident. I have picked the brains of several members of the Ladies Debating Society. I think it was the wife of a Professor of Divinity who first mentioned moles. Her husband, too, is a gardening man, and he has been known to rise at 3am in order to do battle with the little creatures on his own lawn. I'm told that in the season he can be seen in his nightshirt beating the ground with a spade. I told her I needed a topic that was guaranteed to excite the interest of a difficult sitter who was serious about gardening, and she said moles would do it. She was absolutely right!'

CHAPTER 14

*W*hen Vita gave the cab driver the address, he sniffed and made a face. 'I don't go that far out of the city, as a general rule,' he told her.

'Is it so very far?' Vita asked. 'It is still in the city, surely?'

'You might say it was in the city, but to my way of thinking, that's halfway to Royston. The road's muddy and I've had trouble down those old lanes in the past.'

He was a sour-faced man with hairy eyebrows and a flat nose. His coat was so mottled with years of weather and mud that it looked as if it had grown somewhere in the corner of a neglected field. His horse, a wary-eyed piebald, snorted and stamped a foot.

Vita looked along the street to see whether another cab was on its way. None was in sight. 'I could find another driver, perhaps, if it takes you out of your way,' she said.

'I'll take yer,' the driver said. 'But I shall have to stop at the end of that lane. They throw things.'

'Who throws things?'

'The children from those cottages. I was down there last

week with the midwife. There's children there that runs alongside and hurls mud. My old hoss don't care for it,' he said. The old horse tossed his head in agreement.

'I won't be long. You can wait at the end of the lane if you care to,' Vita said, wondering whether it was only the midwife who provoked such bad behaviour, or all visitors.

The horse seemed to lose all energy as soon as they crossed the railway line. It began at a trot, but was dragging its heels in little more than a walk by the time they approached Agnes's address. The driver was right about the mud. The highroad was rutted enough, and the side lane they took after a milestone told them they were four miles from Great St Mary's was a barrier to all but the most determined.

'I'm stopping here,' the coachman called as they neared a public house. 'I shall take a little refreshment at the Cow and Calf. You can find me in the snug by the fire. The place you want is just down there in that row.' He pointed his whip at a row of thatched cottages a couple of hundred yards away.

It was a cold morning, but bright. The track leading towards them shone with puddles, but there was at least a narrow grass pathway between the ruts. Vita, raised in the Devon countryside, had little fear of mud, but knew a treacherous path when she saw one. It was the kind of track that looked a lot firmer than it was and might easily suck the boots off a walker's feet and leave them barefoot and muddied to the knees. Nevertheless, number three Ford Cottages was where Agnes lived, so Vita lifted her skirt as far clear of the mud as she could, and set off.

She was nearing the first cottage, having only once slipped into a puddle that came over the top of her boots, when three ragged children appeared at the front door and glared at her. They were dirty-faced and impudently curious. One, a boy aged perhaps eight years, munched a crust of grey bread. The other two, both girls with matted hair and grimy shawls wrapped around their shoulders, clung to the older boy's muddy jacket. All sniffed loudly and rubbed their noses on the backs of their hands.

'Good morning,' Vita said. The children stared, expressionless and unmoving. 'I'm looking for Agnes Venner's house. Is it this one?' She pointed to the third one along. The three children made no move to reply, so Vita pressed on along the slippery track. Three paces further along she was hit, hard, on the ear by a clod of mud. A peal of laughter rang out and when she looked back, the children were gone and the front door of the cottage was closed.

Feeling hostile eyes on her still, Vita pressed on. Number 3 - there was no identification to be seen, it was simply the third in the row - had a moss-grown thatched roof so thick and low that it left room only for two very small front windows and a front door that was only five feet high. Thin fire smoke was rising from its chimney, so someone must be home. Vita knocked at the door, looking out warily for the return of the mud-slinging children.

It was Agnes who opened the door. She blinked and looked confused to see Vita there.

'Who is that at the door, Agnes?' a shaky voice called from the dark interior.

'I never thought to see you 'ere at my own private home,' Agnes said quietly to Vita. She stood, blocking the doorway. She was not quite as unwelcoming as the children, but it was not far off.

'I wanted to talk to you, Agnes. May I come in?'

'My mother is not well,' Agnes said.

'Who are you taking to, Agnes? Who's there?' The voice behind her called again. It was querulous and beginning to sound anxious.

'Just a lady I know at my work, Mother,' Agnes said, calling over her shoulder. She continued to block the door. Her sleeves were rolled up, and she was wearing an old workaday dress, faded and mended in several places. It was nothing like the tidy clothing she wore at work in Eden Street. 'I don't appreciate you calling on me here, Miss. I'm sorry if that sounds rude, but I have a life of my own and I like to keep it to myself. What I do outside of my work is none of anybody's business. Miss Hazelton has no complaints about my work. I'll thank you to leave me in peace.'

'I'm sorry to trouble you, Agnes, but this is an urgent matter.'

'What urgent matter?'

'Agnes, who are you talking to? Is it a visitor? Can't they come in?' The voice of the old lady called.

'You are unsettling my mother,' Agnes said. 'She is not well. She does not understand things. She is not always quite right in the 'ead.'

'Please, Agnes. I won't keep you long.'

Agnes sighed. She stepped back into the house and held the door. Vita stepped through, ducking her head, and entered the flagstoned interior of the smallest house she had ever been inside. It was dark, but as her eyes adjusted, she could see an old woman in a white lacy bonnet sitting by the fireside in a high-backed chair.

'Is it a friend, Agnes?' the old lady asked, craning forward to peer at Vita.

'She doesn't see well,' Agnes told Vita and added, to her mother, 'Ma, this is Miss Carew, from Eden Street.'

The old lady seemed delighted. 'Oooh!' She cried and clapped her hands together. 'From *Eden Street*! Make the tea, Agnes! Make the tea!'

'The lady won't be stopping,' Agnes said firmly.

'I came to ask you about Albert Flett's room, Agnes.'

Agnes bristled visibly. She picked up the front of the apron she was wearing and began to twist it. 'What about 'is room?'

'When you cleaned the hearthrug, did you find anything?'

'What sort of thing?'

'You moved the rug to clean it, I suppose.'

'Yes. I moved it.' Agnes was looking down at her hands as they worried the apron.

'You didn't find anything when you moved the rug?'

Agnes did not reply.

'She's as good as gold, my Agnes,' her mother remarked. 'Wouldn't hurt a fly, would you, Agnes? Good as gold, she is. Always was. Never mind what people say.'

Agnes still said nothing. She looked down for several long moments, then seemed to shake herself or shiver. 'I'll make some tea,' she said finally.

CHAPTER 15

*I*f there had been another room in the cottage, Agnes would have taken her visitor there, away from her mother, but as there was only one room, all three of them had to sit near the range, Agnes taking a stool for herself, as there were only two chairs.

They were taking tea from Agnes' best china tea cups, taken off the dresser for the occasion. Agnes had selected the only unchipped cup for the guest and held hers oddly because it had lost its handle. The old lady relished her tea with loud slurps and sighs of pleasure.

'I looked in Mr Flett's room again, Agnes, and I found a hiding place under the new hearth rug you had put there,' Vita said.

Agnes concentrated on her tea and did not reply. Her hand was not steady enough to hold the teacup securely, so she set it carefully on the table.

Vita continued. 'It looked as if it had recently been opened. I wondered whether you had noticed the way the floorboards had been cut when you changed the hearthrug.'

'I never saw nothing, Miss.'

'It was difficult not to see it, Agnes. An opening cut into the floorboards right in front of the hearth stone. It was covered by the rug that you moved.'

'Well, I never saw it,' Agnes said, raising her chin.

Agnes's mother watched and listened intently. 'She's 'ad a bit of trouble, but she's a good girl now, en't you, Agnes? Good daughter to me, you are,' she declared.

Agnes was still avoiding Vita's eye, but she reached out a hand and patted her mother's arm.

'All that was a long time ago. We don't talk about those days now, do we, Agnes? That's all in the past. All forgotten,' said the old lady. She gave Vita a twitchy smile. Her boney hands were twisting the strings of her bonnet. 'It wasn't true, anyway. Not a word of it. You tell her, Agnes.'

The old lady's voice was rising. Agitation showing itself in the more insistent twisting of the bonnet strings.

Agnes still did not look up. 'Don't get yourself upset, Mother. It's nothing to worry about.'

'They took her away,' the old lady said quietly. She seemed to be talking to herself. 'I thought I should never see her no more. It was a long time ago. You won't take her, will you? You haven't come to take her away?'

Old Mrs Venner was leaning forward to peer into Vita's face. Her mouth was working and her eyes had filled with tears.

'I won't take Agnes away, Mrs Venner,' Vita said. 'I only want to talk to her for a little while.'

Agnes patted her mother's arm again and sighed deeply.

'I know I did the wrong thing, Miss. I know it was wrong, but I 'ave it still.'

'You found something, then? In the hiding place?'

Agnes nodded her head. 'There was an 'ole. The boards

were loose, and I looked inside and found a tin box. I should've told someone directly I found it, but...'

To Vita's great alarm, tears began to flow down Agnes's flushed cheeks. She turned her head away so that her mother would not see, saying quietly, 'I shall 'ave to go to prison. What will Mother do? There's nobody to care for her now but me.'

'Lovely drop of tea, that is!' her mother remarked. 'pour me a drop more, Agnes, will you?' Agnes wiped her eyes on her apron and re-filled her mother's cup. 'Here? What's wrong with you, Agnes?' The old lady had seen her daughter's tears. 'It's only a bit of tea. That won't do me no harm. Cheer up, gel!'

'How much was there?' Vita asked, speaking quietly in the hope that the old lady might not hear. It didn't work.

'How much what?' piped up old Mrs Venner.

'Don't you worry, Mother. Never you mind,' Agnes reached across to pat her mother's boney hand.

'What money is that she's talking of?'

'Nothing to worry yourself about, Mother,' Agnes said. 'Drink your tea.'

Vita tried again. 'People need to know about it, Agnes, because it will make a difference to how the police investigate Albert Flett's death. They thought he had an accident, but now there are some things about it that point to him having been...'

'... killed. I know,' Agnes said. She turned away and fidgeted with the sleeve of her dress, rolling it up and unrolling it again. 'It was a lot of money. There was a red tin box. I picked it up and shook it, but it didn't rattle. I didn't know if it was money inside, but it had something inside - papers, maybe, or letters. I couldn't see a key, so I finished working on the rug - that was a lot of work. Blood is an 'ard stain to get out. It took me all afternoon, and I left it to dry in the basement passage. All that time I was trying to think what to do about the box. It must be Mr Flett's, but 'e was dead. He had no family anyone knew about. Miss Hazelton often said so. I thought, well what's in it might not be much use, but I might get something for the tin box. People might pay for a tin box. All the time I was scrubbing the bloodstain out of that rug, it was whirling around in my head. What should I do? Should I give it to Miss Hazelton? Should I give it to the policeman? I didn't know. In the end, I took an old knife from the scullery and used it to prize the box open. It wasn't even difficult.'

Vita had waited patiently through this. She was itching to hurry the story along, but Agnes needed to work through things in her own way. The old lady's head fell back in her chair and she closed her eyes in a sudden doze. Agnes rescued the sloping teacup from her mother's hand and put it safely on the table.

Agnes sighed. 'It was full, full of bank notes. A great bundle of them, all folded together.'

'Did you count them?' Vita asked.

'I am fifty-four years old,' Agnes said. 'I'd never touched even a five pound note before that day. Not once. Never imagined touching a ten pound note. Never in all my life. And there were bundles of them. It was too much. It made me feel dizzy. It was too much to believe in.'

'What did you do?'

'It was getting late. Time for me to come 'ome. Miss Hazelton was ready for her supper, but I don't stay while she eats it. I just put it out for 'er before I leave.'

Agnes looked off into the distance and spoke now in as if remembering a dream. 'I brought it back 'ere. Not the tin. I took the tin to Norman Bradley's pawnshop. I thought it

might sell, even without a key. Somebody might have a use
for it. I put the notes into an old potato bag and carried it
home. Then, when Mother'd gone to bed, I took it out and
laid all the notes 'ere on the table and reckoned them all up. I
'ardly knew numbers big enough. There was too much of it. I
put it in piles and counted it all up twice. It added up to a
hundred and seventy pounds.'

'Heavens above!' Vita said, more loudly than she had
intended.

The old lady shifted in her chair and snorted gently in her
sleep. Agnes patted her mother's arm absentmindedly.

'With money like that,' Agnes said, 'I could send for the
doctor whenever mother needed one. We could eat meat and
cakes and fine bread. I could take 'er out in an 'ackney
carriage for a drive in the country, if the weather was good.
New dresses; new shoes. Coal - as much as we needed - for
the fire. We could light the fire whenever we wanted to and
not even 'ave to think twice about it!'

'Where did you put it?'

'I'll never have a chance like that again,' Agnes said.
'Never in all my life!'

'It isn't yours, though, is it?'

Agnes shed another tear and fiercely wiped her eye with
her apron. Her mother snored quietly in her chair. 'I know it
isn't,' she said. 'It's all ten pound notes! There's nowhere I
could spend a ten pound note. They'd think I was mad if I
went into any of the shops I know with a ten pound note.
They'd know for a certain fact that I'd stole it and they'd
send for a constable. I 'aven't been sleeping. I been sitting
here night times worrying about it all. I thought I might take a
note into the bank and ask them to break it down into
shillings, but ten pounds in shillings that's too many to carry!
I've never been inside a bank. They'd take one look at me

and they'd call the constable too. I sat here two nights trying to work it all out, but I can't. I don't even think I want the money any more. And I was afraid of burglars coming in. I never feared them before. We got nothing to steal, not really. But these last two nights I've slept in that chair with a rolling pin in me hand to hit the burglars that come in to steal all these ten pound notes off of me. They'd kill someone round 'ere for a lot less than a hundred pounds, I tell you that!'

'Burglars? What burglars?' old Mrs Venner suddenly piped up. 'What burglars is there, Agnes? I'll get 'em. Give me my stick!'

'There's no burglars, Mother, don't you worry.'

'They shan't have my good brooch without a fight!' muttered the old lady, before going back to sleep.

'Will you tell anyone, Miss? I am afraid of going to jail. Mother would be left alone, or they'd put her in the *workhouse*.' The last word could only be spoken in a whisper, for fear of the old lady hearing the name of a place so universally feared and dreaded by the poor.

'I'll take it to the police and say I found it in Albert Flett's room myself.'

'You won't say it was me what found it?'

'No. There is no need for that. As long as I have it all.'

'I shall never see a sum like that again. It was for my mother and for my own old age, a little coal, a little meat...' Agnes's voice trailed off. She looked towards the fire. 'I wish I'd never seen that dratted money box. It's not as if Mr Flett needed it. He's dead and gone. He don't need it no more! Lord knows 'ow 'e came by it, anyway. It wasn't by honest means.'

'Why do you say so?'

'He was a slippery customer, that one. I always thought so. The mistress could never see it, but I'm sure 'e was leading her on. I reckon he got it by some trickery and hid it there so none of his callers could find it.'

'You don't know that.'

'I don't know, and you don't know neither. This is nothing to do with you, Miss. Excuse me for saying so, but it's true.'

'I saw his body. I was at the post mortem. I am involved.'

Agnes sighed a great sigh and held her head in her hands. 'You won't make off with it yourself and say it was me?'

Vita looked sternly at her. 'Certainly not, Agnes,' she said.

Agnes lurched out of her chair and disappeared behind a door in one corner of the dark kitchen. She could be heard stamping up a creaky flight of stairs out of sight. There was a brief silence, during which old Mrs Venner grumbled indistinctly under her breath, then the footsteps returned and Agnes emerged from the shadows with a crumpled brown paper bag. She dropped it in front of Vita on the table.

Vita opened the folded top of the bag and glanced inside. She could see white notes with elaborate black writing, a great many of them piled together.

'You should count them. I daresay it won't take you as long as it took me,' Agnes said.

'I won't do that,' Vita said. 'I'm sure it's all there. We will not speak of this again, Agnes. I think that would be best.'

'Right you are, Miss,' Agnes agreed. She sighed. 'It's a funny thing, but I feel more cheerful already, now you've got it. Shame about all that lovely coal we could 'ave 'ad though, eh, Mother?'

The old lady only snored in reply.

. . .

VITA CONSIDERED THROWING her own clod of mud back at the children if they confronted her on the way back, but none appeared. The cab driver was still in the bar of the Cow and Calf, and not obviously drunk, so she was soon on the way back to Eden Street with the potato bag on her knee. Vita wasn't sure she had ever touched a ten pound note before, either, so she put her hand inside and did so, but only for a brief moment.

It felt disappointingly like any other worn sheet of paper.

CHAPTER 16

*A*s soon as she entered the parlour, Vita realised there was something odd about the stranger standing by the fire. She had taken off her coat in the hall, and was wondering where to hide the potato bag when she had heard a man's voice in conversation with her aunt. There was no time to carry the bag all the way to her room, so she thrust it into the large Chinese porcelain vase that stood on a windowsill half way up the stairs.

'Vita, this is Mr Henry Longbridge,' her aunt said, as her niece came into the room. 'He has called to see you. I was just telling him that I knew his aunt when she was part of the Ladies Lecture Society.'

There was a look in her aunt's eye that Vita found difficult to interpret.

'How do you do?' Vita said. 'And please accept my condolences.'

Longbridge stood and shook Vita's hand with a hint of hesitation. He was wary. 'Yes,' he said. 'It was a great shock.' He did not look directly at Vita as he briefly grasped her hand, frowning and turning his head to one side instead.

An awkward silence fell over the room as the two ladies waited for this unexpected caller to explain his presence.

'Perhaps you would care for a cup of coffee, Mr Longbridge? I often take one at about this time,' Aunt Louisa said. She gestured him to take a seat, but he made no move. 'Or perhaps a sherry. If it is not too early in the day for you. You may prefer it, especially on a cold day.'

Longbridge threw himself abruptly into the chair. 'I have lost something,' he blurted out. 'Something very important.'

'I'm very sorry to hear that,' Louisa said. She pressed the button over the mantelpiece to summon Tabitha, still giving the same significant look to Vita.

The ladies were both on the sofa opposite Longbridge. He was tall and slim, with a mop of hair falling forward on his forehead. His face was lean, with small, hooded eyes surrounded by dark shadows. His clothes were well made, but rumpled, and his shoes were muddy. A button was missing from his waistcoat. In all, he had a preoccupied and distracted look.

'I came here, you see, because I want you to help me.'

'Of course we will help you in any way we can,' said Aunt Louisa with a gentle smile. She pressed the button again.

'I think it is Miss Carew who can help me.' Longbridge turned and fixed Vita with a look of such sudden intensity that she felt her heart thud.

'Certainly,' Vita said, imitating her aunt's calm tone, 'I shall help if I can.'

Longbridge shifted so that his whole body directed itself towards Vita. His face was pale. 'You have been in the room of an acquaintance of mine, Albert Flett, I believe.'

'Yes. Miss Hazelton sent for me when the maid first found Mr Flett.'

'Did you take anything?'

'I beg your pardon?'

Longbridge rolled his eyes in instant irritation. 'Did you *take* anything from the *room*?' His voice was louder than good manners allowed, its tone sharp and impatient.

'The police were there,' Vita said. 'There was a police constable with me.'

'Police!' Longbridge muttered in a tone of disgust. 'What good did they ever do? Now you listen to me, Miss Carew, I believe you have taken property from Albert Flett's room that is not yours to take. I want it returned. I shall take steps to retrieve it unless you hand it to me now.'

Louisa pressed the button a third time. 'Do you presume to threaten my niece?' She said. 'You must be upset, Mr Longbridge. I cannot allow you to… '

He whipped round in the chair, facing Louisa now, but pointing a trembling finger towards Vita. 'Your niece is a thief and a liar. She is intent on creating trouble,' he said.

TABITHA ENTERED the room carrying a silver tray with a coffee pot and three cups. Longbridge's pointed finger together with the atmosphere in the room were enough to stop her in her tracks. After a brief hesitation, she set the tray on the sideboard and dropped a curtsey. 'Chef would like a word, Madam,' she said. 'There is a difficulty with the menu.'

'Send him up immediately, please.' Louisa replied.

Longbridge ignored this. He was rigid in his chair. 'I *know* you took something,' he told Vita, leaning suddenly forward to spit his words into her face. She could see a glistening chain of saliva between his lips and feel his hot breath. There was strong drink on it.

Louisa stood suddenly. 'Mr Longbridge, I'm very sorry,

but there appears to be an urgent matter I must discuss with my chef. I hope you will excuse us, but we simply must deal with this. I will show you out myself.'

Smiling, Louisa gestured an invitation to Longbridge to stand and precede her out of the room. He glared at Vita for a moment longer, then leapt to his feet and stalked out, his movements jerky with irritation.

Vita heard the front door close before her aunt returned to the parlour with a hand pressed to her bosom and sank back into her chair. Vita hurried to the sideboard where the sherry decanter was kept and poured her aunt a generous measure. Louisa was just lifting it to her lips, when the chef and Tabitha hurried back.

'Not to worry, Monsieur, Tabitha, our unpleasant visitor is gone.'

'I thought he was a strange one,' Tabitha said. 'He was terrible rude to me on the doorstep, earlier. Nearly elbowed me aside. I never thought he'd be rude to you ladies too. He's that one in the papers. I seen his picture.'

The chef, elegant in his long white apron, had thoughtfully brought a large cleaver with him. He continued to hold it ready.

'Thank you Monsieur Picard. And you, Tabitha. I imagine the problem in the kitchen was your own invention?'

'It was, Madam. I didn't like the look of that gentleman,' Tabitha said. 'I hope I did the right thing.'

'You certainly did. Vita and I are grateful. I don't know that he would have resorted to anything violent, but he was certainly angry and bullying in his manner.'

'It is some madman, *non*?' Monsieur asked. 'I should call for the police?'

'No need. He was just an unexpected and ill-mannered visitor,' Louisa said. 'One must make allowances, I suppose.

He is recently bereaved, but to come here making allegations against Vita, well!'

'He speaks against Miss Carew?' The chef's hand tightened on the handle of his cleaver.

'Yes, something about the death of that unfortunate young man who stayed with Miss Hazelton. But for now, he is gone, thanks to your quick thinking, Tabitha, and your speedy response, Monsieur. Have you ever deployed that weapon, by the way?'

Monsieur flexed his hand on the cleaver's ebony grip. 'I am a chef, Madame, not a Barbarian. In the great houses of this country, I have several times encountered people who richly deserved a taste of my sharpest blade, but I did not think them worthy of my attention!' He turned on his heel. 'Mercifully, my *sauce* is undamaged by this man's impertinence. A house of ladies is not safe with madmen like this free to walk the streets of Cambridge.'

Or free to climb the rooftops of the city, either, Vita thought.

CHAPTER 17

*V*ita took a single sip, then set her cup down. 'I will be a little late for luncheon, Aunt, if you will forgive me. There is an errand I must run.'

'Alone?' said her aunt in alarm. 'When that man might be outside, waiting?'

'I need to go to the police station.'

'Can it not wait until after luncheon, dear?'

'I'm afraid not. I must deliver something.'

Louisa looked at her niece piercingly over the top of her little silver spectacles. 'I did observe - when that dreadful Longbridge man was here - I could not help but notice that you did not answer his question.'

Vita looked at her feet. 'No, Aunt, because I did take something from Albert Flett's room. The postcard.'

'Oh yes, I was forgetting the strange postcard. Is that what he was after?'

'I can't say for sure. Anyway, there is something else. I did not take it, but it has come into my possession.'

'*Come into your possession.* You sound like a witness in the Police Gazette!'

'It's money. Quite a lot of money.'

'Oh dear,' said Louisa.

'A hundred and seventy pounds.'

'Oh, good heavens! And you found it in his room? What's a young man like Flett doing with an amount like that? That is more than three times my fee for a college portrait!'

'I didn't find it, Agnes did.'

'Agnes the maid?'

'Yes.'

'She stole it?'

'No, she found it and didn't know what to do with it. It's possible that she considered stealing it, but she handed it to me willingly enough. She lives in very poor conditions, Aunt. I was shocked. A dank little cottage miles away, with her poor elderly mother. '

'She has the look of a woman whose life has been hard, I always thought so. But she gave the money back, you say?'

'Yes. I have it.'

'You have it? Where?'

'In the Chinese vase on the stairs.'

'Oh, my word. I'm very glad I did not know that when that dreadful man was here just now.'

'I had no idea he would just come to the door in that way.'

'No. So now you want to take the money to the police?'

'Yes. It seems best to get it out of the house.'

'I agree. But I certainly do not agree to your carrying it through the streets alone. Could you not summon a constable and ask him to carry it away?'

'I would not like to entrust it to someone else's hands, Aunt. Constable Williamson is a perfectly honest man, as far as I know, but some of the others are not so incorruptible that a large sum of money in ready notes might not go astray.'

A sharp rap at the front door made both of them jump. They looked at one another anxiously. The caller knocked loudly once more. Tabitha appeared in the hall.

'Shall I answer, Madam?' she asked, 'Monsieur will be here shortly, but he did not want to leave his sauce.'

'Ask who is calling,' Louisa told her. Tabitha called the inquiry from behind the door and a cheerful voice replied.

'Derbyshire here! Open up, Tabitha. A man could perish for cold on this doorstep.'

ONCE THE STRANGE visit from Henry Longbridge had been explained, Aloysius Derbyshire forgave the chilly welcome.

'Why, that is the very reason I came, to warn you about him,' he said. 'I have just had a conversation with one of my pupils who knows him well, and who said Henry Longbridge was behaving in an odd and alarming way since his aunt died. My pupil's rooms are near Longbridge's and he heard him pacing the floor all night long last night. He was talking, raving and raging, but he seemed to be alone. He seems not to be eating or attending lectures. Some of the students believe he keeps a gun in his room. It seems to me that he might be suffering from a nervous attack of some sort.'

'Brought on by grieving the death of his aunt, do you think?' Aunt Louisa said.

'I doubt that,' said Derbyshire, 'he was notoriously scathing about his aunt among his friends. I'm told he kept the print of a huge pig hanging in his rooms and used it for dart practice. He had painted the name Henrietta Longbridge on its frame and paid a shilling to everyone who scored a bullseye by landing a dart in its nose.'

Aunt Louisa's hand shuddered as she raised her sherry glass to her lips. 'The insolent young pup!'

'So, if it is not grief that is distracting him, it must be something else,' Vita said.

'Shame, perhaps, or remorse for treating her with disrespect while she was living?' Louisa suggested.

'Or he had a plan and something went wrong. Something he is worried about.'

'A mysterious plan and an unexplained death - how very exciting!' Derbyshire exclaimed, rubbing his hands together. Vita and her aunt both looked at him with stern disapproval.

'Oh, come now! She was a dreadful woman by all accounts and he is an extremely unpleasant young man with dissipated habits who stands to inherit a fortune - who would not be fascinated if such a pair of gargoyles were at odds? *I* certainly am! It said in today's paper that she was found by the butler at the foot of her own stairs. I for one shall be lapping up every detail.'

'It is not a game,' Vita told him. 'We are forgetting poor Albert Flett. He may have been caught up in something that got out of hand.'

'Flett is the young man who lived with our neighbour, Mr Derbyshire. They called for Vita when he was found,' Louisa explained.

Derbyshire looked a little ashamed. 'Forgive me, ladies. I was allowing myself to be carried away. I should not be taking a thoughtless delight in others' misfortunes. Although, in my defence it is only human to be extremely curious in such cases, as Vita's interest confirms. They would not print special editions of the newspapers unless people were eager to read of the unhappy events in the lives of others.'

'That does not make it...'

Another loud knock at the door interrupted; the beating of the doorknocker prolonged and strident.

'Good heavens! Who is that?'

They crowded into the hall, but Tabitha was already opening the door.

It was Inspector Llewellyn with no fewer than three burly constables. After the briefest explanation, they overruled all objections and began to search the house. It took only a few minutes for the youngest officer to plunge his hand into the Chinese jar as he passed it on the stairs, and find the potato bag that Vita had hidden.

'I am afraid I shall have to charge you with theft, Miss Carew,' the Inspector told her, once Vita admitted that it was she who had put the money there.

'But I explained. It was found in Albert Flett's room and I was intending to bring it to the police station this afternoon.'

'You appeared to be enjoying a social morning and about to eat a rather delicious lunch,' remarked the senior police officer, stroking his moustache. 'I see very little sign of your hurrying to hand these funds in.'

'I would not let her go. It was my fault, officer,' Louisa put in. 'Henry Longbridge was so threatening in his manner earlier. I did not want my niece to venture out alone.'

'I came to accompany her, as a matter of fact,' Derbyshire added. 'I am an accomplished swordsman.'

'Very impressive,' said Llewellyn. 'The fact remains that Miss Carew has obtained a large sum of money that is not hers and has secreted it. It is all very well to say that she was going to hand it in.'

'Who told you to come here?' Vita asked.

'I am not at liberty to disclose that,' Llewellyn said.

'It was Henry Longbridge, wasn't it? He left this house, walked directly to the police station and accused me of theft! The bounder!'

'You have acted extremely promptly, if that is the case,' said Louisa. 'You have jumped to attention for Mr Longbridge. There was no such diligence in the investigation of poor Albert Flett's death, if I may say so.'

'That is neither here nor there. You are conflating two unconnected cases.'

Llewellyn's earlier manner had lost a little of its confidence.

'But there are connections. Plenty of them.' Vita told him.

'That remains to be seen. I suggest my officers accompany you to the police station immediately,' Llewellyn told her. 'Come politely, or I shall ask Constable White here to use his handcuffs.'

The excitable young constable fumbled at his pocket to find the handcuffs, dropping a pencil and his whistle in the process.

'Handcuffs? You are surely not serious?' Aunt Louisa cried.

'No, Aunt, do not be concerned. Handcuffs will not be needed. I will go willingly. It will be easy to set matters straight,' Vita told her. 'I shall be back as quickly as I can. And I have four members of the police force to protect me from Henry Longbridge on the way.'

CHAPTER 18

*O*nce they were in his office, Lewellyn settled himself at his desk after poking the fire until it roared. His constable sat in a corner with a notepad at the ready and Vita was made to sit on the worn chair Llewellyn's suspects were all offered - its seat so sagging that the stuffing had sunk inward, forcing her to perch in great discomfort on the angular wooden frame.

The trophy collection of the Cambridge constabulary had its home in the shelves behind the Inspector's desk, along with the annual photographs of his men standing to attention in tiered and helmeted ranks, every button shining, every face proud, solemn and bearded. Vita removed her glasses, which had steamed over in the warm office and polished them on her skirt.

'Now, young lady,' Llewellyn said, 'I believe this is the second time I have spoken to you in this office. I hope you do not mean to make a habit of involving yourself in crime and criminal activities.'

'The allegations made against me were false last time and they are false now too, Inspector,' Vita told him.

'Am I to make a note of this, Sir?' asked the young constable.

'Yes, Constable White, write her statement word for word, if you please.'

'Yes, Sir.'

'Kindly explain to me how the money came to be in the china jar, Miss Carew.'

'It was found in Albert Flett's room and...'

'... who found it?'

'Does that matter?'

'It certainly matters, Miss Carew.'

'I would rather not say who found it.'

'You did not find it yourself, then?'

'No, I found where it might have been - a hole under the rug, but there was nothing there.'

'Someone else had already taken it?'

'Yes.'

'Someone you will not be naming?'

'Yes.'

The Constable in the background leaned closer to his notebook, scribbling in the attempt to keep up.

'I have the power to arrest you for non-co-operation, Miss Carew.'

'But I am here, co-operating, surely?'

'You are refusing to tell me who found the money?'

'If you have the money now, what difference does it make?'

'What difference?'

'Yes!'

'You are refusing to co-operate with an officer of the law!'

'I *am* co-operating, Inspector! I have handed you the money that was found hidden in Albert Flett's room. I have told you where it was. It is one hundred and seventy pounds. It is all there, contained in the paper bag your officer found in the jar.'

'I don't take kindly to being patronised, Miss Carew.'

'I am not trying to patronise you in the least, Inspector. I want only to hand in this money in the proper way.'

The Inspector rested his elbows on his desk and pressed his fingertips together in a steeple as he eyed the irritating young woman before him. The fire crackled and when it fell silent, they could hear the junior constable's pencil still scraping in the background.

'How do I know that you did not hit Albert Flett yourself because you wanted to make off with his money? For all I know, you might be the murderer.'

'How could I have killed him?' Vita asked. 'I was called after the maid and Miss Hazelton had already found him dead.'

'Why did they send for you and not a policeman?'

'They sent for me because I live next door and am known to have a little first aid training. Agnes ran for a policeman at the same time and found Constable Williamson on the corner of Fitzroy Street. He was there ten minutes after I arrived. I had time only to check Albert Flett's pulse and listen to his chest. I had scarcely concluded that he was dead before Williamson was there. You were there yourself within half an hour. Williamson and I searched the rooms for any clue that might explain what had happened. We found nothing at all except an old postcard.'

'Where is that old postcard now?'

'I have it at home.'

'At home? You made off with a piece of evidence?'

'I put it in my pocket. I simply forgot about it. It didn't seem important.'

'I'm told you also went to the post mortem examination.'

'Yes, I did.'

'It is not a public spectacle, a post mortem. Why did you wish to attend? It seems very unsuitable.'

'I am studying science and anatomy in particular. I have been present at the photographing of a post mortem examination before and I have begun dissection classes. I thought it would be interesting to attend.'

'Interesting? Many people would think of it in different terms. Most young women I know would be horrified and sickened by such a thing.'

'As I said, I have seen dead bodies before. I did not think I would be shocked by seeing Albert Flett examined. I was right; I found it interesting, not frightening. And I was able to ask the Police Surgeon a number of questions myself. He confirmed that Albert Flett was probably punched on the jaw before hitting his head.'

The Inspector closed his eyes and shook his own head in disbelief.

A knock on the door distracted them. It was a sergeant who stepped in, saluted, and stood to attention.

'Yes, Sergeant,' Llewellyn said. He sounded weary.

'We counted the notes, Sir. One hundred and seventy pounds exactly.'

'Thank you, Sergeant. Put it in the safe, please.'

The sergeant saluted and left.

'I believe that Henry Longbridge hid in the roof space while we were in Albert Flett's rooms,' Vita said. 'He is an expert climber. I think he hid in the roof space and listened to everything that was said. Then he waited until everyone left and prized enough slates from the roof to climb out and down the drainpipe. The builder who repaired the slates found only two had fallen down from the roof. Another twelve or so were in a tidy pile inside the roof space. I think he had to kick a small hole first, but after that, he was able to reach through and pull the other tiles off one by one. He had all night. He did not even need to worry about how long it took. Once the hole was large enough, he climbed down the drainpipe and made off.'

The Inspector's demeanour shifted a little when he listened to this. Vita noticed that the police constable had stopped writing and was looking at her in surprise. She wondered what it was she had said to hold their attention in this sudden way.

'Excuse me for a moment,' the Inspector said. 'Stay with her, Constable.'

He stood and left the room. He did not hurry - that would not have been suitable to his rank, but there was a certain determination.

The coal in the fire hissed and shifted in the grate.

'I wonder why the Inspector left so suddenly,' Vita said, voicing her thoughts aloud.

'It might be that he has heard about people climbing roofs already today,' Constable White replied. He then frowned and added, 'I shouldn't have mentioned that, I suppose.' He was a fair-haired young man without a beard, which would make him stand out in the heavily bearded ranks of next year's Cambridge Constabulary photograph.

'Are you a new recruit?' Vita asked.

'Yes, Miss. Six months into my probation.'

'That's why we haven't met. I took First Aid classes with the probationary constables, but it was more than a year ago now.'

'With Doctor Goodman? I'm doing those now. Reviving the Drowned it was this week.'

'Ah yes, Reviving the Drowned - pumping the arms up

and down, putting them over the back of a horse and making it trot! Does the doctor still use the same small boy for bandaging practice?'

'I believe so. Young Anthony Dodds. He must be the most bandaged boy in Cambridge. He told me he was paid a shilling a time. A shilling! No wonder he's always willing.' The constable chuckled.

'Yes, there can't be many boys who have received as much First Aid as Anthony. I enjoyed the classes a great deal. I am studying science now. I hope to train in medicine. It was all started by Dr Goodman's classes.'

The Constable was about to answer when Inspector Llewellyn abruptly returned.

'You can go, Miss Carew. I have no cause to detain you longer.'

'You no longer plan to press charges against me?'

'There has been a development in another case far more serious.'

'In the case of Lady Longbridge's sudden death?'

Llewellyn took a deep, slow breath, drawing in as much patience as he could with the inhalation. 'See Miss Carew out, Constable White, if you please. And Miss Carew, I would advise you again not to involve yourself any further in matters that are rightly the business of the police force and the police force *alone*. Meanwhile, I am prepared to accept your rather partial explanation of how you came by the money, and to accept that the sum found was, in fact, £170. It might have been ten times that amount, for all we know, and you might have made off with the difference!'

'It was £170, and I have given it all to you,' Vita said.

'Goodbye Miss Carew!'

'Oh but...!' Vita began, but Constable White had risen and taken her arm, and now he led her firmly out of the door.

CHAPTER 19

*A*lone figure slipped out of a shadowy doorway as Vita came down the steps of the police station. She paused, catching her breath, but it stepped into the lamplight and revealed itself to be Aloysius Derbyshire.

'I did not mean to startle you. Your Aunt has asked...'

'Oh, Mr Derbyshire, surely not! Surely my aunt does not fear me walking home from the police station alone. It is hardly ten minutes' walk.' Vita strode ahead.

Derbyshire trotted to keep up with her. 'But, who knows what forces of evil lurk across Parker's Piece, waiting to kidnap young women and carry them to Bluebeard's castle, or into slavery in Brazil? Quite apart from the awful Longbridge!' he called.

'*Slavery in Brazil*!' Vita snorted. 'What utter nonsense! I have just been released from the most irritating interview with the police. Now, kindly make way, I am in no mood for tomfoolery.'

'I'm willing to bet the Inspector decided there was no charge to answer and thanked you for your public spirited action in returning the money,' Derbyshire called, still hurrying to keep pace.

'You are half right. No thanks were offered. He seemed suddenly to want to get rid of me as quickly as possible. A titled lady dies in odd circumstances, and Llewelyn immediately drops everything else. There must be a new development in that case, I think.'

'How fascinating! I wonder what it was?' As usual, Derbyshire made no attempt to conceal his gleeful enjoyment of the tragic news story currently monopolising the Cambridge headlines.

'He sprang up as soon as I told him that I believed Longbridge had hidden himself in the roof after Albert Flett died.'

'In the roof?'

'I think he hid in the eaves because there were people coming and going in Flett's room. He could hear what they were saying. He waited until night, then pushed his way out through the roof and climbed down the drainpipe.'

A pair of young men on bicycles passed them. One balancing a large music instrument - a cello, perhaps - on his handlebars.

'Perhaps someone did the same at Miss Longbridge's house!' Derbyshire suggested, relishing the idea.

'Mr Petit would know. He knows all the roofs in Cambridge. I shall ask him.'

'Of course,' Derbyshire went on, 'Longbridge may not have needed to break in or out of his aunt's house. He might have had a key.'

'No, they had a falling-out. He was in her bad books.'

'Well then, perhaps a servant let the nephew-gone-to-the-bad in. Perhaps he offered the butler or the housekeeper a juicy bribe! Or, if he was such an expert climber, which I doubt - he is a lazy beast and his muscular strength was not impressive when I worked with him - he might easily have let himself in at a window. There are a great many windows to choose from.'

'This speculation is not helpful.' Vita said. 'Although, now you mention it, perhaps they suddenly realised they had checked everywhere in the house but the roof.'

Vita came to a sudden halt and turned to face Derbyshire.

They were half way across Parker's Piece, standing under an ornate lamppost which stood at a crossroad of several paths. The other people about were hurrying, muffled against the cold. 'It would only require a short diversion to walk past the Longbridge house.'

'Your aunt would certainly insist I accompanied you.'

'My aunt will not know!'

'I shall accompany you, none the less.'

'Oh well, if you insist. Derbyshire, is that a *sword stick*?'

He raised the ordinary-looking cane with a smile, but made no reply.

IT WAS A COLD, damp evening. Derbyshire, prompt and energetic, but well-wrapped, swung his sword stick as they took the route over a misty Jesus Green. They crossed the river and approaching the house on Chesterton Road so that it loomed over them from the hill above. It was only about thirty years old, and although constructed of modern red brick, it had many ancient castle-like touches in its fashionable architecture, including a castellated turret and several stained glass windows. The vast arched front door was studded with ironwork resembling a portcullis, with the name of the house 'Langcraggs' carved into a brick shield above. From across the road, where they stopped in the shadow of a college wall, there were a number of downpipes clearly visible, but it was becoming too dark to see much else.

'Henrietta Longbridge lived alone, I believe,' Vita said. 'Apart from her servants, that is. I saw two of them, a man and a woman, when I met her in the street once.'

The windows at the front of the house were shuttered. The whole building looked cold and lifeless.

'I shall return in the early morning,' Vita said. 'It will be easier to examine the house in the daylight.'

'At seven?' Derbyshire asked.

'Yes.'

'I shall call at Eden Street at a quarter to seven, in that case. It means only a short diversion from my usual morning run.'

Derbyshire turned, as if that concluded arrangements.

'I am perfectly well able to come back alone, Mr Derbyshire.'

'As I say, I shall call for you at a quarter to seven. Now we should return to your aunt before she raises the alarm. She will wonder why you are so late.'

AT SUCH AN EARLY hour on a frosty November morning there were few people out, but the boathouses were already open along the river. Hardy rowers were calling to one another as they carried their eights down to the water's edge and climbed in. Their breath steamed around them.

Derbyshire, well-muffled, but wearing short running trousers, ran on the spot every time they stopped to cross the road. Vita found this irritating, but there was no shaking him off.

They paused opposite Langcraggs, to take in its shuttered bulk. There were many downpipes as well as all manner of dormer windows, ledges and brickwork decoration that Vita imagined a climber could use as a foothold.

A man with a dog on a lead came out of one of the houses a little further along Chesterton Road. The dog was excited at the prospect of an early run in the park. It tugged its owner towards the footbridge over the river, but not before he had spotted Vita and Derbyshire and come over.

'If you're from the newspapers, you can get along home,' he said. 'We've all had enough of your sort sniffing round night and day.'

'We are not reporters,' Vita told him.

'Well, if you're just nosey sightseers, you should be ashamed of yourselves,' the man said. He was struggling with the dog, which, being a large Labrador, was strong enough to make its wishes clear. 'It's a disgrace, the way people come and stick their noses in when something bad happens.'

'It must have been very upsetting. Were you a close friend of Lady Longbridge?' Vita asked.

'Me?' The man looked surprised. 'No. No indeed. We were neighbours, nothing more. Grand lady like that - her house is five times the size of ours. She wouldn't have much to do with the likes of us. Except to complain. She set the lawyers on my other neighbour over a tree in the garden. Pigeons sat in it, she said. She couldn't abide them, so my neighbour was to cut down the tree! She complained about Laddie here barking. Or rather, she sent that man of hers to complain.'

'Timpson? Is that the name?' Vita asked.

'That's the one. Timpson. Very high-and-mighty he was.'

The dog walker paused and looked up at the house with them. 'I told the police, Laddie barked a lot that night. The night she died. Barked and barked. They didn't take much notice. I suppose a dog barking isn't worth writing down.'

'What made the dog bark?' Vita asked, 'Did you see anything yourself?'

'I'm short-sighted. I saw nothing. But the dog was looking up towards the roof and barking his head off. I couldn't stop him. He's a good dog, as a rule. Aren't you Laddie?'

The dog wagged his tail, agreeing, but still tugging his owner towards the park.

'He would bark if he saw somebody climbing on the roof of the Longbridge house, perhaps?' Vita said.

'Could be. I thought there might be a pigeon up there, or a squirrel. Laddie hates squirrels. But it could have been a man, now you come to mention it. I won't tell the Mrs. She can't sleep for worrying about what happened. We wouldn't feel safe in our own beds anymore if it weren't for Laddie here.'

The dog pulled again, and the man gave in and allowed himself to be hauled along to the footbridge that led to the park.

He had only just released the dog and let it run off joyfully along the riverbank when a pair of police officers approached Langcraggs.

Vita and Derbyshire stepped behind a coal cart which had pulled up to make a delivery on their side of the road. They watched as the officers entered the garden of the house and walked around it, apparently examining the outside. They pointed up at the roof and one of them made notes.

'They are wondering whether someone hid in the roof here, too, I should say,' Derbyshire declared. 'You see! You gave them that idea.'

After several more circuits of the house, the officers knocked at Langcraggs' great front door. They knocked several times before anyone opened it. The shutters were still closed. Eventually, after an extended discussion on the doorstep, the policemen were admitted.

'I wonder why they have returned?' Vita wondered.

'Perhaps the butler did it!' Derbyshire said, grinning and starting to run on the spot again.

Vita glared at him. 'This is all just a jolly game to you, Derbyshire, isn't it?'

CHAPTER 20

*T*hey looked at the house for a moment longer, then the bell of St Giles's church chimed eight times. Vita jumped.

'Oh no! I shall be late for the post mortem! Underhill invited me to Miss Longbridge's post mortem, but he insists on punctuality.'

'Where is it to be held?' Derbyshire asked.

'Old School Lane - the laboratory!' Vita was already beginning to hurry in that direction. 'I cannot be late! It is a great privilege to be invited.'

'Come along then,' Derbyshire said, breaking into a run. 'I'll be your pacemaker. Keep up!'

Vita could only pull the hat from her head, pick up her skirts and run after him as fast as her legs would take her. The streets were lively with a workday morning's traffic. They dashed along the pavement at such a speed that pedestrians leapt aside, dawdlers stopped to stare and mothers tutted and clasped their babes close to protect them from the hurtling pair. They wove together across streets clogged with carts and cyclists, skirted handcarts and hawkers on the pavements, swung themselves round corners on lampposts, leapt puddles and dodged deliverymen carrying sacks to the shops.

By the time they reached the door of the laboratory, Vita was too breathless to thank him, and could only leave Derbyshire panting at the threshold, while she darted up the stairs pausing only at the door of the post mortem theatre to compose herself with a single ragged breath before attempting to slide into the auditorium as noiselessly as possible.

Luck was not on her side. As she closed the door, her skirt caught in it. Not noticing, she stepped forward, but it jerked her off balance, throwing her onto her knees and pitching her spectacles forward into the aisle.

A shuffle of interest passed around the observers seated on the raked seats. Several young gentlemen looked over at the fallen latecomer, and Dr Underhill, who had been addressing them with a question about the deceased's appearance, broke off and glared.

Vita, on hands and knees, felt helplessly around for her lost glasses. Her hair was loose on one side and she was still out of breath. The whole audience, three rows of dark-suited University men and half a dozen police officers in uniform, looked on coldly, until at last one merciful police sergeant stepped from the front row and helped her to her feet before retrieving the glasses. Still attempting invisibility, she nodded thanks, put the glasses on, pulled her hair behind her ears and looked about her for the nearest seat.

Underhill, however, had other ideas. 'Oh no! Do not presume to take a seat, Miss Carew. If you cannot be on time, you cannot have the privilege of attending my post mortem. You lack respect. That is my final word. Leave now. You are a disgrace to Newton college and to the reputation of all women students. Leave now, I say!'

Every pair of eyes in the auditorium returned to Vita, who had no choice but to stumble back out the way she had come.

In the empty corridor outside, she leaned against the wall to recover herself. Tears of frustration and rage more than self-pity flooded her eyes. *The public humiliation! The injustice!* She dashed her sleeve across her eyes, hearing footsteps approach, then went back to the door. Could she hear what Underhill was saying from there? she wondered.

'The lady students go in the cleaning cupboard, usually, when they're locked out,' a voice said from behind.

The speaker was a middle-aged woman in an apron. She carried a broom and gestured for Vita to follow her, as if the procedure were perfectly routine. 'You can't hear so much at that door, but from in here...' she led Vita round a corner and opened a door hidden in the wood panelling. It was completely dark inside. '... from in here, right at the back, you can hear everything, and they say that if you stand in the right place, you can even see through the cracks in the boards and get a good enough view. That's what the lady students tell me, anyway. It's a bit dusty, but the other ladies never seem to mind.'

Vita looked at her in amazement, but the cleaner only put her finger to her lips and, ushering her inside, closed the cupboard door behind her.

It was pitch dark at first, but Vita's eyes adjusted, and she found herself standing in the space underneath the raked seating of the post mortem theatre. Spaces between the planking meant she could see the legs and shoes of the students who had stared at her. She slid along until her line of sight was better and was rewarded with a clear, but partial, view of Underhill and the body on the examination table.

Underhill was addressing the onlookers. 'We come now to the issue of the exact cause of death. A corpse which has fallen - and this lady, as you know, was found at the foot of a staircase - is generally assumed to have died as a result of that fall, but assumptions are not our business. It is cold, objective facts that we must gather, Gentlemen, in order to assure ourselves, and everyone concerned, that this person did not die of some other cause either before or after they fell. Death may take place after a fall, but be caused by something other than the injuries thus caused. So, how should we proceed? Any thoughts, Mr Perkins?'

Vita heard the unfortunate Perkins hesitate before suggesting, 'By a general inspection of the external body, Sir?'

'Observing what, in particular?'

'The colour?' another voice asked timidly.

'Yes. And what else? Come *on*, gentlemen, or we shall be here until doomsday!'

'Abnormal disposition of the limbs?' someone called.

'But before that?' Underhill said impatiently. 'Gentlemen! You must not overlook the facial expression. The facial expression in a drowning, as a random example,' he continued, 'is usually calm. Our subject here does not have a calm look. What we see expressed here is anxiety, at the very least - one could even say fear. The skin is pallid, the lips blue. Suggestive of what?'

'Syncope,' someone said.

'Yes. Sudden cessation of the heart from fear, or some other cause. Our examination of the heart itself will establish whether you are correct, Mr Clegg. It is always important to examine the mouth for foreign objects. All orifices of the body must be examined - why is that, Mr Clegg?'

'Anything left unexamined may be implicated as the cause of death in court,' the unseen Clegg replied.

'In a drowning, there could be waterweed or plant material. Oh. But in this case...'

Underhill paused and Vita, with her partial view, could only imagine that he was examining the body's mouth. There was silence from the observers, as if they were leaning forward to scrutinise whatever it was he had found. Vita willed someone to describe it, but Underhill just resumed his former tone and continued, 'We will, of course, come to the contents of the trachea and bronchial tubes in good time.'

Settling herself in the dusty cleaners cupboard, Vita watched Underhill continue to guide his observers through the methodical process of the post mortem. It was odd, she thought, to have seen Lady Longbridge in life. The cadavers Vita had worked on in dissection classes were partial, and therefore deceptively anonymous. It was difficult to imagine them alive. Her Ladyship's personality seemed somehow much more present. She was also a far more fleshy body than Vita usually encountered. The uncomfortable realisation dawned on her, as she stood in the dark, that the corpses the medical school offered students were almost exclusively the bodies of the poor. They came from workhouses, prisons, or even the hangman's noose. The corpse of someone who had lived a comfortable, wealthy life - even if their death had been sudden - was a rarity in Vita's experience so far.

CHAPTER 21

*a*unt Louisa looked her niece up and down in furious
indignation. They were standing in the hall at Eden
Street, Vita having just arrived home after the post mortem.

'You look as if you fell through a hedge backwards!
Whatever happened to your hair? And why are you covered
in dust?'

'I had to hide in a broom cupboard.'

'Tabitha! A sherry please. Come in and sit down, Dear. A
broom cupboard? Why?'

'In order to see the post mortem examination of Lady
Longbridge.'

'Vita, it can't be good for you to witness these horrors day
after day. You will give yourself nightmares! What would
your father say?'

'My father is of a scientific frame of mind, Aunt, as you
know. I imagine he would find it all very interesting.'

'Take a little sherry, Vita. It is good for the heart.'

'But it makes my nose as red as a tomato!'

Her aunt waved this objection away. 'Only the first glass,
dear. After that it settles down. You left early this morning.'

'I went to look at Lady Longbridge's house, to check something first, and then I remembered the post mortem and Mr Derbyshire…'

'I'm glad Mr Derbyshire was there. He offered to act as your guard.'

'I need no guard, Aunt, I can assure you. But, as it happens, he was most helpful in running with me to the post mortem. I was afraid of being late. I was still late, and the Professor was annoyed and refused to admit me, so I had to hide in the broom cupboard. It wasn't too bad. Lady students often use it, apparently.'

'Good heavens! You watched a human body dismembered from inside a broom cupboard? It all sounds more and more like the kind of cheap novel I would strongly advise any niece of mine to avoid!'

'It was magnificent, Aunt! Absolutely fascinating. The miracle of human anatomy revealed in a post mortem examination! The internal organs have a sort of functional beauty - oh, it is hard to explain. It is thrilling, quite simply thrilling! And Dr Underhill was so skilful and carefully accurate!'

'This is the gentleman who threw you out?'

'Yes. He is a wonderful teacher. Each process described and explained, each organ painstakingly examined and its secrets revealed. The heart, for example…'

'I think that is enough detail for now, dear, thank you.'

'It was a great privilege!' Vita said, absent-mindedly sipping her sherry.

'A privilege to watch from inside a dusty cupboard?'

'Well, it was extremely embarrassing to be sent out of the room at the beginning, but I was late. I was in the wrong.'

Aunt Louisa sighed and patted her niece's hand. 'Luncheon is ready. And we have guests for dinner tonight, remember?' She led her niece to the dining table, where

Tabitha was ladling soup. 'It might be better not to talk too much about your morning's activities over dinner tonight, Vita. Many guests prefer to avoid the subject of dead bodies while they eat. There will be some medical men present, and we must try to keep even them off unsuitable topics as well. I have put you next to Mr Pottendale, the organist. He might be hard work, but I hope you won't mind making conversation with him - gardening always works well, and I believe he has an interest in church architecture as well. You have the rest of the afternoon to browse the encyclopaedia for conversational hints. And, Vita dear, there is something crooked about your spectacles again.'

It was not church architecture that inspired Vita that afternoon. Instead, she spent it reading Grey's Anatomy, making notes about the post mortem procedures she had witnessed; the intricate structures of the body, and the methods used to uncover its delicate secrets.

As, later, she changed hurriedly for dinner and tried to put her gingerish hair into some sort of order, her mind returned to the odd scraps of information she had discovered about Henry Longbridge: he visited Flett; his aunt was very wealthy; he was a gambling man; he was a night climber. He might have hidden himself in the roof of Miss Hazelton's house, but he did not steal Flett's money. Perhaps he did not know it was there? Perhaps he had no interest in the money? He was heir to a fortune, so perhaps a hundred and seventy pounds was of no interest to him? He urgently wanted *something* from Albert Flett's room.

The slivers of information refused to come together in any useful way.

She sighed at her reflection in the dressing-table mirror.

No amount of brushing could rid her hair of the dust it had accumulated under the raked seats of the post mortem theatre. Efforts at straightening her spectacles had not been successful either. She looked a fright. The best she could do was to dab a little cologne onto her wrists and hope the company would be so beguiled by Monsieur's food that they paid her defective appearance no attention. It wasn't much of a plan, but it might work.

The sound of cheerful company was already rising from the sitting room as Vita came downstairs. She was turning over in her mind the topics of gardening and church architecture that might be useful with Pottendale over dinner, and did not at first notice the figure hesitating in the hall.

'Ah!' he said when he saw her. It was Pottendale himself, partially concealed behind a potted palm.

'Hello, you are Mrs Brocklehurst's most recent sitter, I think. Mr Pottendale, isn't it? I am her niece, Vita Carew. Will you come into the drawing room?'

'How d'you do?' the gentleman said. They shook hands. It was an awkward moment, he staying at his outstretched arm's length and withdrawing his hand rapidly. 'How did you know me?' he asked.

'I have seen your portrait in the studio.'

'Oh,' Pottendale said. His tone was difficult to assess, but roughly speaking, it was one of hopelessness. His shoulders sagged.

'Surely it has not been as bad as all that, Mr Pottendale?' Vita said, hoping to jolly him along. 'Most of my aunt's sitters seem to enjoy the process.'

'A nightmare,' he said, looking away. 'It has been a nightmare. Being looked at. Being *scrutinised* for hours at a time. I would frankly rather have my teeth pulled.'

Vita wanted to sympathise, but a small emotional dam

had broken inside the celebrated organist and he now burst forth.

'It certainly wasn't my idea to have a portrait made. It was the college. I have been there a long time. It is a tradition. The reason I play the organ - the reason I was drawn to it in the first place, is because I am alone. I sit up in the organ loft away from everyone. I have it all to myself. I abhor company. Any kind of social engagement is a kind of torture for me. I often find myself like this. In the hall. Unable to step into the next room when it is so full of people. All enjoying themselves. Laughing, and so on.'

Vita found herself wondering why, if he expected such torture, Mr Pottendale had accepted the invitation.

'You are wondering why I troubled myself to come,' he said, reading her thoughts. 'I accept because, well, because I trust and hope that one day I shall overcome this - this appalling hesitancy. I have no wish to be a recluse. I do not, in point of fact, despise people or disdain company. I only find myself, somehow, out of my natural element.'

'A fish out of water?' Vita suggested.

'Exactly that! I am a fish, as you say, out of water.'

Both wondered what to do next for a short time, as the laughter and cheerful talk swirled around the next room.

'I could make your excuses for you, if you simply want to leave,' Vita suggested.

'That would be cowardly,' he said. 'I have come this far.'

'I could go in ahead of you, and act as a diversion while you slip into the room behind.'

'Or, you could take my arm and guide me in.'

'I could.'

'Will you find me a seat in a corner?'

'Yes, I can certainly do that.'

'Forward, then!' Pottendale said, in the manner of

someone leading a very quiet cavalry charge. He drew himself up and offered Vita his arm.

Vita took it and together they entered the room, where they attracted only mild interest, and where the celebrated musician was soon settled in a chair half-hidden by a fire screen, a position he very much approved.

As she turned away, Vita almost stumbled over Dr Goodman, standing by the window.

'Ah, Vita!' he said, 'I believe you already know my colleague, Dr Underhill.'

'We have met,' Underhill said. 'I am delighted to see that you are not late for *every* occasion, Miss Carew.'

Vita could only manage a watery smile, before she was saved by Tabitha sounding the dinner gong.

CHAPTER 22

*V*ita's prayers to be sitting somewhere far away from Dr Underhill at the table were answered. She found herself between Pottendale, who now considered her an ally, and the solicitor, Victor Waring. *Why had her aunt invited Mr Waring?* Vita wondered.

'You were most kind to my mother the other day,' he remarked, as the soup was cleared and the trout fillets brought in.

'I hope her hand is healing well,' Vita said.

'Very well. And she need no longer fear for our vases, since poor Lady Longbridge will no longer be visiting the office.' He ate a piece of fish without looking particularly mournful.

'She was a regular visitor, I gathered.'

He nodded. 'The details of her will were a constant preoccupation. It is only to be expected in the case of a single lady with a large fortune and very few relations.'

'A nephew was mentioned in the newspapers,' Vita said, carefully.

'Yes. The nephew. That is not going to be straightforward.

She wrote him out of her will recently – I am giving no secrets away here, she was perfectly happy for it to be public knowledge. She discovered that he had a reputation as a gambler and a drinker. She was so furious that she stopped his allowance and would have taken an advertisement in the Cambridge News and disinherited him publicly, if I had not I advised against it.'

'She particularly disliked gambling?'

'She abhorred gambling and strong drink, and had discovered that her nephew was passionately fond of both.' The lawyer took a sip of his wine. 'To be frank, there had been rumours about him in the family for some time. It wasn't entirely a surprise.'

'She disinherited him?'

'Yes, immediately, as I said. But since then there has been what you might call a 'rapprochement'. Young Henry has mended his ways. He has abandoned his bad habits, become a regular church-goer and by all accounts even improved his studies.'

'And did this tempt his aunt to re-instate him in her will?'

'It would be quite improper for me to confirm or deny such a thing, as of course you know,' Waring told her, but he was smiling as he said it. 'This trout is quite delicious!'

Aunt Louisa leaned forward to address the solicitor from her seat at the head of the table. 'Miss Hazelton tells me that you have a fine baritone voice, Mr Waring. I hope you will favour us with a song or two, after dinner?'

'With pleasure,' Mr Waring said.

'Oh good heavens, not music!' muttered Mr Pottendale, sitting on Vita's other side. He was hunched over his plate, as if trying to make himself disappear. She turned to him. 'You will not join in the musical part of the evening?' she asked.

'I dread that above all things,' he said, addressing his plate.

'But you perform every day in public, and often to large audiences,' Vita reminded him.

He sighed over his fish, and added in a desperate whisper, 'from the organ loft! *Out of sight!*'

'Mrs Goodman is our usual accompanist. She enjoys it.'

'Someone will feel obliged to ask me. They always do.'

'Not tonight. I shall see to it.'

The organist relaxed a little and took a bite of his dinner. 'You think me an old fool, I imagine.'

'Nothing of the sort. Let us change the subject. Do you live nearby?'

'On Chesterton Road, not far from the river.'

'Ah, so you would know Langcragg's House.'

'I walk past it daily. Sad events there, lately, I read. Why do you mention it?'

'Would it be easy to climb onto the roof, do you think? If one were a climber of a decent level of skill?'

'What sort of question is this?'

'I was just wondering,' Vita said, eating a forkful of *pommes dauphinois* as nonchalantly as she could.

The organist seemed to consider the question, or perhaps he was considering Vita's motives for asking it, but either way he answered after a while. 'It must be possible because I have seen people up on the roof on several occasions. I am a church warden at St Giles's on the corner. The churchyard overlooks the house. I lock the church in the evenings, usually on my way home from college. I generally walk around the outside to look out for anyone sleeping in the churchyard before I lock the doors. I have a clear view of the roof of Langcraggs from there, and I have several times seen workmen up there. Lady Longbridge had netting installed - to prevent pigeons nesting.'

They both ate for a moment more. And recently?' Vita asked.

'There was someone up there only the other day. I saw a flock of pigeons sent up. Somebody frightened them off. It would have been about five o'clock. I thought it was dangerous, putting someone up on the roof when it was already almost dark, but Lady Longbridge detested pigeons, all the neighbourhood knew that. She would go to any lengths to keep them off her roof. She complained endlessly that they nested in the church. They do, naturally. She had a morbid fear of the things.'

'YOU DID sterling work with Mr Pottendale,' Aunt Louisa said, as they closed the doors behind their final guests later. 'I do believe I saw the man smile once or twice.'

'He is simply very shy, I think,' Vita said. She had caught sight of her reflection in the hall mirror and was attempting again to straighten her crooked spectacles. 'I was surprised to see Victor Waring among the guests. Do you know him?'

'Not directly, but Delia Goodman knows him through the Amateur Operatic Society. I thought it might be useful for you to have a word.'

'Aunt! Are you collaborating in my investigation?'

'In general I disapprove. But in this particular case I did think I might be of assistance.'

'Thank you. It was most helpful. Both my dinner neighbours provided useful information, as it happens.'

Louisa smiled. 'I am rather good at dinner parties,' she said, 'though I do say it myself. I must go and have a word with Monsieur before he leaves. That trout was superb, and he likes his efforts to be acknowledged. Oh, I nearly forgot. Did Dr Underhill speak to you?'

'No. I am very glad to say that I avoided him successfully all evening.'

'He left a note for you on the hall table,' her aunt said, as she left to find the chef.

CHAPTER 23

*V*ita took the note up to her room, speculating more pessimistically with every stair about its contents. Would it be a sharp refusal to allow her ever to enter a post mortem laboratory again? Would it be a warning that her college would be informed of her gross lack of punctuality? Or, even more dreadfully, was it a dire comment on her performance in the viva exam?

She sat on her bed and looked at the envelope scrawled with her name. The handwriting was angular and spidery. She turned it over and looked at it this way and that for fully ten minutes. Then, unable to put the evil moment off for any longer, she grabbed her paper knife and cut the envelope open.

The jagged scrawl on the crisp paper inside read:

Dear Miss Carew,

I hear from your aunt that you found the broom cupboard. From there, I know, the view is imperfect. I am accordingly enclosing a sketch made by my laboratory technician of the foreign body I picked out of the deceased's oral cavity. The police officers present found the object unremarkable, but it might be of interest to you.

Yours,

F. Underhill

The little sketch enclosed was an exquisite scientific watercolour. It appeared to show the same object in two states. First matted, damp and dark; then cleaned and dried. Damp, it was a merely a clot of twisted fibres, but once dried it became a short, fluffy feather, downy, soft-looking and pale blue-grey.

Vita peered at the image intently. Lady Longbridge hated and feared pigeons, yet she had died with what looked very much like a pigeon feather in her mouth.

～

BY SEVEN THE NEXT MORNING, after a night of only fitful rest, Vita was back on the street outside Langcraggs. She had already visited St Giles's churchyard, and as Mr Potterton had said, there was a clear view of the side and part of the rear of the building from there. She could also make out the nets which had been stretched over some of the ornamental brick-work and ledges to prevent pigeons from landing, but these were incomplete. In several places they had either been blown off by high winds, or were missing for some other reason.

It was a cold morning, and the chill was making Vita feel pessimistic. Once again she was looking for something, but not sure what it might be. She was walking opposite the house, with the river on one side and a few early carts and bicycles passing, and about to go home for a warming cup of tea, when a crash and a sudden shout nearby made her turn on her heel.

A cyclist - a young woman - had taken a tumble. Vita ran over and helped her to her feet, righting the cycle.

'Oh, how stupid!' the rider said, irritably shaking mud off her skirt.

'Are you hurt?' Vita asked.

'No. Only annoyed. The rope caught in the spokes. I should have taken more care. I train my volunteers to carry ropes safely, and here I am breaking my own rules. No-one to blame but myself.'

She had a rope coiled over one shoulder and began winding the loose end back into the coil and fastening it. Vita recognised her.

'You're Miss Robinson. I saw you at the gymnasium. I am Vita Carew. Edward - your self defence instructor - is my brother.'

Miss Robinson looked up from her rope and smiled. 'How do you do. But you can't call me Miss Robinson. I am Adelaide. Please call me that, or Addy.'

'You are up and about very early,' Vita said.

'You are too! I'm on my way to the boathouse for early rowing practice.'

'With a rope?'

Adelaide smiled. 'I borrowed it from the boat house for the volunteer fire brigade at college. We were training. Are you heading for the river? Perhaps you have early rowing practice too?'

Vita shook her head. Something about Adelaide's straightforward and hearty manner made Vita tell her the truth. 'I was just looking at this house. I'm trying to work out whether it would be possible to climb up the outside of it.'

Adelaide expressed no surprise at this mission, but looked briefly up at the big house. 'Yes, I should think so. Personally, I would use the flat roof over a bay window. If there's one at the back, that would be perfect. Why?'

'Are you a climber? You sound as if you know what you are talking about.'

Adelaide shrugged. 'I've tackled a few peaks in the Cairngorms - nothing special.'

'You know that the resident - Lady Longbridge - died suddenly?'

'Yes. I read about it.'

'I have a suspicion that it might be connected to the sudden death of our neighbour. Nobody will listen to me. I thought if I could prove that a suspect could have climbed up and entered the house, or even have climbed down after hiding in the roof, they might pay attention to my suspicions.'

To her credit, Addy looked unstartled by this. 'The suspect you have in mind, would he or she be fit enough to climb?'

'Yes. The person I'm thinking of is a night climber, I'm told.'

Addy looked back at the looming red brick building. 'Then such a climb should have presented no difficulty at all, I would have said. Shall we try it ourselves?'

'Try to climb it?'

'Yes. It is still early, nobody will see, if we are quick.'

'I can't climb! I've never even tried.'

Adelaide shrugged. 'It's easy enough. You have decent co-ordination. You are fairly strong. You've probably climbed trees before now. I'll show you what to do.'

'What if we're caught?'

'We won't be. I'll leave my bike here by the wall. Come on, follow me.'

Without hesitating, Adelaide crept along the wall, darted across the road and ducked behind a hedge on the drive of the house. Appalled at what she was doing, but also thrilled, Vita hurried after. They followed the hedge up to the front of the house, staying out of sight of the windows, and then dashed from cover over to a low side gate. It was open. Once in the back garden they tiptoed beside a fence to the corner of the building, where there was a large metal down pipe.

'Could you climb up to that?' Addie whispered, pointing to the flat roof above a large bay window about twelve feet up.

'No!' Vita said. 'How?'

'Follow me,' ordered her companion, and began to scramble up the drainpipe before Vita could argue. It took Vita several tries - the pipework was freezing cold and slippery - but she finally climbed far enough off the ground for Addy to reach over and pull her up onto to the flat roof. They crouched there to catch their breath. A decorated ironwork balcony ran around the back of the building about eight feet above their heads. There seemed to Vita no way of reaching it, but Adelaide had other ideas. She threw the end of her rope up and pulled it through the iron railing before knotting it round her waist. 'I'll let it down for you when I get there. Duck down below the windows, we don't want to be seen by anyone inside.' Then, by some gravity-defying method which completely mystified Vita, she half climbed and half walked up the wall and over onto the balcony. The rope swing down and hung in front of Vita.

'Tie yourself on!' Addy called down in a stage-whisper.

Vita made some attempt at this, not remembering any of the knots her father had taught her, but ending up with something reasonably secure. The rope then tightened, and she hauled herself up the drainpipe on one side with Adelaide's assistance from above. There was a horrible moment where she was required to let go of the pipe and allow herself to swing in mid-air, but somehow, breathless and desperate, she managed it, and found herself crouching on the balcony. Adelaide gave a brief smile before detaching the rope from Vita's waist and coiling it.

'Do you learn this sort of thing as a volunteer fire officer?' Vita gasped.

'Of course! How else would we rescue someone trapped on an upper floor? Now, what exactly are we looking for?'

They both looked along the ironwork balcony. There were three large sets of windows, and along at the far end, a much smaller one set high in the wall. 'I'm not sure,' Vita said. 'I want to know whether someone could climb out through the roof after making a hole from the inside.'

They both leaned out and craned their necks to look upward, but the roof was another floor higher and had an overhang. It was impossible to see.

'Why would someone hide in the roof?'

'I think that's what he did at my neighbour's house. And then climbed down in the night and got away.'

'It would be just as easy to hide out here on the balcony, I'd have thought,' Adelaide said.

'Would it be possible for someone to reach up to that small window at the end?'

'It's a bit high,' Addie told her. On hands and knees she crawled in that direction, staying underneath the windowsills. Vita could only follow. 'Oh no, look. Someone has conveniently put a box there to climb on.'

She was right. A stout wooden box had been placed underneath the window. As they crawled along, Vita could see something beside it. It was a crowbar.

'Could someone climb through that window?' she asked Adelaide.

'It's small. I don't think so. It's probably a bathroom.'

'It has been prized open, to judge from the marks on the frame. Probably with this.' Vita showed Adelaide the crowbar.

'Yes. That would do it. But why open it if nobody could climb in?'

'Perhaps something was to be handed out?'

Adelaide looked unconvinced.

Vita looked up at the window, and then a thought struck. 'The balconies and ledges around all have netting on them. To keep the pigeons off. But this one does not.'

'No. There are feathers everywhere, look!' There were. Small downy feathers had been blown into every corner. There were several trapped behind the box. Vita picked one up. It was very similar to the one Underhill had found.

'Someone laid pigeon traps here, perhaps,' Adelaide said.

'The owner of the house hated pigeons. Really hated and feared them. That's why she had the nets put up. Adelaide, I think someone climbed up here and put a pigeon in through that window.'

'To frighten the poor woman deliberately?'

'To frighten her to death. And it seems to have worked.'

Adelaide was about to reply when a window was suddenly thrown open further along the balcony. Both women crouched and held their breath. Someone was moving around inside the room. They could hear footsteps and later the sound of a fire grate being vigorously cleaned.

'We should go,' Adelaide said quietly. 'It's easiest to go straight down here.' She nodded towards a long drainpipe that ran from this end of the balcony straight down to the ground, a drop of about twenty feet onto paving stones. 'I'll help you reach across the space and go down first. Then, if you fall, you'll fall on me and have a softer landing.'

It was a joke, but one Vita was in no fit state to enjoy. She found it difficult even to look straight down. 'I don't think I can,' she said.

'You'll be right as rain, Vita, but now we must cut along before anyone spots us up here. Leave the crowbar. It will better evidence if it's seen as you found it.'

With that, Adelaide pulled Vita to her feet, climbed over the handrail of the balcony and reached across to the down-pipe. It was a gap of about six feet. She leapt it without hesitation and stretched her arm back encouragingly.

Vita stared at her, unable to move.

'Come along, Vita. Don't waste time thinking about it, just leap. I will catch you.'

A sash window was thrown open further along the balcony. Both women froze as a feather duster emerged and was vigorously shaken.

'Vita, come on,' Adelaide whispered.

It is impossible, Vita thought. *She will not catch me. I will fall from her grasp, plunge down, break limbs and possibly my neck. I may die. I may be killed as a result of the stupid idea I had of finding out about...*

'Vita. Don't think. Jump!'

So she jumped.

CHAPTER 24

It was difficult to explain why they were laughing so hard. Several cyclists gave the young women curious looks as they sat by the river on a cold bench, rocking and wiping away tears of laughter, their breath clouding around them.

'Your face was a picture!' Adelaide said.

'I thought I was going to die!'

'I'd have caught you.'

'How can you be sure? It was a long way down!'

'Well, I'd *probably* have caught you, and we couldn't stay there. Anyway, did you find what you hoped for?'

'I think so.'

'What will you do?'

'Tell the police. They should listen this time. I have evidence, thanks to you.'

'Is it enough? It's clear that someone was there, but not who it was.'

Vita stopped laughing and frowned. 'You're right, I suppose. The church warden from St Giles' saw pigeons put to flight. A neighbour's dog barked and looked up at the roof

143

of the house, but I don't suppose that's enough. They are just circumstantial things. Wait! The crowbar will have finger-prints on it.'

'Did you touch it?'

'No.'

'Neither did I. That's good. Is that enough?'

'It might be. I'm not sure. Perhaps he wore gloves.'

That stopped them both.

'The man you suspect. Is he a violent character?' Adelaide asked.

'He is ill-tempered, certainly. I'd guess he was capable of violence.'

'You should take care, Vita.'

'He knows I'm taking an interest in Albert Flett's case,' Vita said. 'Perhaps I should ask my brother for training in Oriental Self-Defence.'

'Stand up,' Adelaide said suddenly.

'Why?'

'I'll show you how to escape a strange hold. It was this week's lesson. Grab me round the neck from behind.'

'Like this?'

'No, harder. Use your whole arm.'

'Like this?' Vita put an arm around Adelaide's neck, the crook of her elbow tight to the throat.

'Yes. That's it. Tighter. Now watch.' Adelaide sank down by slackening her knees, then jabbed her own elbow back and up so that the point of it caught Vita in the ribs. 'If you do that hard - that elbow jab - it will knock the wind out of them. Or you could stamp as hard as can on a foot. I hope you won't need any of that, but you never know.'

'Won't you miss your rowing practice?' Vita said, remembering.

'Oh dear, yes. I'd better go.' Adelaide stood and grasped the handlebars of her bike.

'Thank you, Adelaide. I'd never have climbed the house alone.'

'It was fun! I'm sure we'll meet again. Good luck, Vita. Let me know if you need to be hauled up any more buildings!' Addy climbed onto her bike and with a brisk wave, pedalled off along the bank of the river towards the boathouses.

VITA LONGED FOR A HOT BATH, but knew such an extravagant request would scandalise her aunt. Only duchesses took hot baths during the day. She settled instead for a wash to remove the grit from her hands, and a good brush of her skirt and jacket. Climbing was damp and dirty work. Her skirt and boots bore the scars, and she had somehow managed to graze her nose.

Over breakfast, Louisa quizzed her niece about her dawn outing, but accepted a vague explanation. She was too busy anticipating a lecture that evening. 'Can't I persuade you to come, Vita? It's *Ancient Remains of the South West* tonight; Stonehenge and so on. Fascinating! Professor Lewis is the most riveting speaker. I saw him on *Standing Stones of the North* last year. It was quite marvellous!

Vita sipped her tea and hoped her Aunt would change subjects so that she wouldn't have to make an excuse. Standing stones held very little appeal at that moment.

'I have had a letter from your father, Dear,' Louisa went on. 'He plans a visit! And soon. That is something to look forward to, anyway.'

'Yes, it will be good to see him. This visit is quite unexpected, at least to me.'

'He is a little concerned about your studies. I suggested a visit to reassure him.'

'He has not mentioned feeling concerned in his letters,' Vita said, adding marmalade to her toast. The excitement of the morning had given her an appetite.

'I may have mentioned your difficulties over anatomy, and so forth.'

'Did you tell him about the anatomy test?'

'I may have. I assumed you would already have told him yourself.'

'I have not. I was ashamed, frankly.'

'There is no need to feel ashamed, Vita. I am told it is quite common to re-take an examination paper or two. Didn't your brother do so?'

'He did, but it adds to the expense. There are extra fees. Papa is hard pressed as it is.'

'Oh dear,' said her aunt. 'I had not thought of that.'

'Many students take private classes, or pay for additional dissection time.'

'Have you considered doing so yourself?'

'I have considered it, but I cannot afford to pay. The instructors charge extra for women.'

'To teach the same material? Why do they do that?'

'They consider us harder to teach. And we can only gain access to the laboratories and dissection rooms out of hours. The university is pressed for space.'

Her aunt looked at Vita over her reading glasses. 'Does the university know about this practice of charging women students extra?'

'I imagine they do.'

'How much extra do these tutors charge, exactly?'

'Four times as much, in some cases.'

Her aunt's teacup froze in mid-air. 'Good Heavens! That is an outrage. I shall have to have a word with someone.'

'With who?'

'With *whom*, Dear. I'm not sure, but the lecture tonight will be a good place to start. The wives of half the professors in Cambridge are sure to attend. I shall mention this injustice at every opportunity. Are there no scholarships or bursaries available? I'm sure I've heard of such things.'

'Only for those who perform outstandingly well. I am most definitely *not* eligible.'

'That seems the wrong way round to me, Vita. Surely it is the students who find their studies most difficult who should be awarded scholarships? I shall mention that tonight as well. Well, Dear, don't be downhearted, it will be a pleasure to see your father. But I must hurry. Our friend Mr Pottendale will be here soon for his final sitting. The portrait is transformed. Between us we have breathed life into the man. His eyes very nearly twinkle!'

houghts of her father quizzing her on the progress of her studies led Vita to spend the day in the Newton college library. With the anatomy exam over, she returned to the other subjects that persistently haunted her: mathematics and physics.

It was a long, restless day, not helped by the uncomfortable chill of the library. A single fireplace offered only a meagre fire which warmed a six-foot radius, only to make the rest feel even colder. Newton students knew to wrap themselves in coats and blankets, so the few others Vita could see working at the tables had only their faces and fingers exposed and were otherwise just shapeless mounds of warm fabric. By four o'clock, with dark falling outside, Vita was stiff and her brain refused to take in another single word of a textbook, so she gave in and returned to Eden Street.

She had long ago overcome her first instinct, which had been to rush to the police station to share her thoughts about the pigeons and the crowbar immediately with Inspector Llewellyn. Recent experience told her that this would only cause him irritation. Instead she returned to her room and set about compiling her notes into a clear dossier. Calmly presented with documented evidence, Llewellyn would surely have to act, she reasoned. Even if he wanted to reject her ideas, he would have to look into them first.

She hoped that once he saw the evidence she had put together, he would arrest Henry Longbridge without further ado.

As she re-read her notes, however, she had to admit that there were obvious blank spots. Firstly, how did Henry Longbridge come to know Albert Flett? Why did he visit him? If he did punch him on the jaw; why?

The only shared interest between them seemed to be horse racing. Flett's form book proved he knew the racing world, and Longbridge had a reputation as a gambling man. A reputation that his aunt had taken such exception to that she cut him out of her will. Perhaps they were simply gambling friends?

Why would gambling friends fall out? A disagreement over winnings? An accusation of unfair dealing? An unexpected loss? A debt?

Vita knew so little of horse racing that she could hardly imagine how the matter of placing a bet on a horse was even undertaken. Did one approach a jockey? She had heard of bookmakers. Who were they? Where did one find them?

But, on the other hand, perhaps it was coincidence that Flett and Longbridge both bet on the horses. What did she know about Albert Flett? He had a useful sum of money hidden - a generous amount, but certainly not a fortune. He was not employed by Bainbridge's, but he paid his rent punctually. So where did his money come from? If it wasn't from gambling, perhaps it came from something else. His commercial art? Did he paint posters? There was no sign of posters being designed at his attic desk. There were only two sketch books with most of the pages removed. And that odd little postcard.

Vita sighed, frustrated, and looked out of the window at the winter garden, darkening in the late afternoon. Something caught her eye - a movement in the hedge at the far end, but she was too far away in her thoughts to dwell on it.

The postcard was where she had left it, propped against her looking glass. She stood to pick it up, but passing the window, the same movement near the hedge at the end of the garden once again attracted her attention. There was something there.

Sleet was falling, and the air, when she opened the window, was icily cold. She heard a sharp little cry. It seemed to come from the end of the garden, where the large sycamore was illuminated by the street lamp in the alley behind. It sounded like an animal.

Vita hurried down the main stairs, pulling her coat off its hook as she passed the hall and taking the lower set of stairs to the back door near her aunt's studio. Out in the garden she waited, wondering if she had imagined the sound, but after a moment or two it came again; a sharp *miaow*. She followed the sound until she was under the branches of the tree, and there, crouched in the cover of a twisted root, she spotted Minmou. The poor cat was a sad remnant of her usual friendly self. Her fur was matted and wet and she seemed unable to stand. All she could do was to look with huge eyes at Vita and utter her sad cry again.

'Minmou! Poor thing!'

Vita stooped to reassure the frightened animal, but as she did so her arm was gripped from behind and viciously twisted behind her back. A voice she immediately recognised as

Henry Longbridge's spoke quietly into her ear. 'Keep quiet. Cry out and I will break your arm.'

The pain in her shoulder was sharp and mounting. She gasped, but did not scream. 'What do you want?'

'I want you to stop poking your nose into my business. You are meddling in things you don't understand.' His lips were pressed against her ear. As he spoke he jerked her arm higher. 'Stay out of this. Do you understand me?'

Vita was breathless with the pain. Her knees were almost giving way beneath her. 'Yes. Yes, I understand what you want.'

'And will you? Will you stop this meddling?'

'What made you punch Albert Flett?'

Vita regretted asking immediately. Her captor's reaction was to throw his other arm tightly around her neck and squeeze until she felt the pulse pound under the pressure.

A long moment of silence followed, during which damp snowflakes fell on Vita's face. She could hear Longbridge breathing, smell the damp on his tweed sleeve and feel his hard cheek against hers. Part of her was terrified into helplessness by the overpowering strength of his grip, but another part of her brain hunted about, trying to remember what Adelaide had told her. *Elbow - rib - foot - stamp. Anything to get my breath back!*

Sagging at the knees, which pulled Longbridge off balance, she stamped her boot onto his left instep at the same time as poking her left elbow backwards with all the strength she could muster.

An outraged yell of pain was Longbridge's reply. He lost his hold, but only for a moment. Before Vita could get away, he had her arm twisted behind her back again.

His ragged breathing was in her ear. The pressure on her

neck even harder. 'You vicious bitch. I could squeeze the life out of you right here and now.'

The night was suddenly pierced by a strange wailing. The haunting howl of a cat; sharp, loud, eery and prolonged, rang out around them. A terrible keening. It surprised Vita that a little injured cat could make such a noise, much less keep it going, one howl following another in waves echoing around the shadowy garden.

Longbridge's grip loosened a little on Vita's neck. He cursed the animal and tried to pull Vita toward Minmou's hiding place, intent, she guessed, on kicking the cat into permanent silence.

But the back door was already open and Louisa and Tabitha, alarmed by the extraordinary yowling, both hurried down the garden path, calling the cat's name.

In an instant, Longbridge dropped Vita and disappeared into the hedge. She caught a final glimpse of his tall figure clambering over the wall, followed by a thud and another curse as he landed badly on the other side.

AT FIRST, all attention was on the cat. In the warm kitchen Minmou was wrapped in a blanket and set in a basket near the range. Tabitha fed her drops of milk and water while Louisa gently examined her.

'She seems weak, but I can't find any broken limbs,' she said, straightening up. 'I'm no expert, but I think she might be expecting kittens. Vita, you are as white as a sheet!'

'You are, Miss,' Tabitha agreed. 'Are you poorly? Here, sit yourself down.'

'In the garden...I was - somebody grabbed me from from behind. He twisted my arm and seized me round the neck!'

'What? Here in the garden? Are you hurt?'

The two other women both looked horrified.

'No, I think I am alright now. My shoulder is a little sore.'

'Tabitha, fetch Vita a glass of brandy!'

'It was Henry Longbridge. He wants me to stop meddling.'

'You should get the police after him,' Tabitha said, pressing a small glass into Vita's trembling hand. 'Shall I go and find an officer? Evan - Constable Williamson, I mean - is not on duty tonight, but there should be someone on the beat nearby.'

'No,' Vita said.

'Whyever not?' asked her aunt. 'That young man's a menace. Attacking a young woman in her own garden at night, indeed! He should be thrown into prison.' Louisa urged the glass to Vita's lips.

Vita gave in and took a sip. It made her cough. 'It shows, doesn't it, that I must be on to something? He wouldn't bother to come here threatening me, if he wasn't worried. I've spooked him.'

'Vita, the brute is willing to use force on an innocent woman! Spook him any further and he might do something much harsher than twist your arm!'

'I must know something, or have something that incriminates him,' Vita said, 'I wish I knew what it was.'

'You must tell the police! Whatever would your father say if he knew his daughter was assaulted by a ruffian - to say nothing of her having attended the scene of a crime and a post mortem examination.'

'Two post mortem examinations, actually,' Vita said.

'Even worse!' cried her aunt. 'My brother will think me outrageously irresponsible for allowing you to involve yourself in such matters. I can hardly even imagine what he would say.'

'I'll tell the police by noon tomorrow, Aunt. Please let me wait until then. It will give me a few more hours to try to work out why Henry Longbridge is so worried.'

Her aunt looked doubtful, but then conceded. 'Noon,' she said. 'No later.'

'Oh!' they heard Tabitha exclaim. She was peering into the basket at Minmou. 'Look! A kitten!'

There was, indeed, a wobbly, damp little scrap of a kitten next to Minmou in the box.

CHAPTER 26

'Come, Vita, I'll help you to your room. Rest is what you need, my girl,' Louisa said. 'The kitten will still be here in the morning.'

'There'll be more than one, I expect,' Tabitha said, leaning over the box, 'dear little thing. I shall take the box up to my room, Madam, if you'll allow it. I can keep an eye on them up there.'

Vita had left the postcard from Albert Flett's room on her desk. Her aunt, after leading her upstairs and poking the bedroom fire into life, picked it up. She peered at the postcard and ran her finger over its surface once or twice before looking up sharply. 'This is not a real stamp,' she said.

'It looks real to me,' Vita said, adjusting her spectacles and looking over her aunt's shoulder.

'It is not a stamp at all. It is the *painting* of a stamp. Someone has painted a stamp onto a postcard.'

Both women examined the stamp closely by the light of the fire. 'Look, the artist has painted a fold in the perforations and even the tiny fibres where the perforations have been torn. He has given it an entirely three-dimensional effect by adding the narrowest shadow down one side. It's a trick. A tiny trompe l'oeil. And very skilfully done too.'

They both stared the postcard and the stamp, admiring the effectiveness of the deception.

'Is the postmark real?' Vita asked.

'Yes, I think it is.'

'But, Aunt,' Vita said. She was still looking at the postcard. 'Why would anyone go to such trouble? It saved them only a penny, and it must have taken a very long time to paint something so convincing. '

Aunt Louisa frowned, 'I have heard of this kind of thing. I know someone who might be able to tell us more. He lives nearby. He is an interesting character, Vita, you'll enjoy meeting Corry.'

'Corry?'

'Short for Coriolanus. Coriolanus Long. His father was a Cockney coal merchant who loved Shakespeare. His sisters are Ophelia and Cordelia.' Louisa laughed. 'Monsieur Picard is off tonight, but no doubt Tabitha will find something to tempt Corry's appetite. He is very fond of his food, as I recall. I shall call on him immediately.'

'But, Aunt, it is dark already. I should go instead of you.'

'I wouldn't hear of it,' Louisa said. 'You rest here for half an hour. I shall speak to Tabitha about dinner, if I can distract her from Minmou and the kitten for long enough, that is, and be back by six o' clock. '

'I'm not happy about you going out alone, Aunt. Longbridge is out there.'

'He has no interest in me. Besides, I shall take my umbrella. I once fought off a very determined pickpocket with that umbrella,' her aunt declared, '*in Paris*!'

'Even so,' Vita said. 'I shall come too. He would not risk attacking two of us together in public.'

'I might attack him, though, if I see him first, the *scoundrel!*' cried Louisa.

In the event, they both went, and it was an uneventful errand. Puzzlingly to Vita, they did not walk to the gentleman in question's home, but to the public house on the river called the Fort Saint George, where her aunt left a note with a barman. The pub, apparently, acted as Coriolanus Long's place of business.

'LOUISA BROCKLEHURST! The finest portrait artist this side of Rome! How are you? A sight for sore eyes, as ever!'

The man on the doorstep raised a brown fedora he had been wearing at a jaunty angle. He went on booming merry greetings as his overcoat was removed, revealing a green tweed suit, yellow waistcoat and red necktie. He had a generous brown moustache and unruly hair, which was determined to stick out at the sides, despite being thoroughly oiled. He looked to Vita like the sort of man you see at country fairs, bargaining over horses, but he spoke with a definite Cockney accent. Not the usual sort of guest at her aunt's dinner table, certainly.

'And 'oo is this loverly creature?' he asked, turning with a smile to Vita.

'Corry, may I present my niece, Vita. She is here to study at the University.'

'Is she *indeed*?' cried Mr Long, warmly shaking Vita by the hand. He sounded delighted.

'Vita, this is Mr Coriolanus Long. He is an art expert and adviser to several major collections and museums.'

'Delighted,' Vita said, experiencing a handshake from Mr Long that felt like one from a kindly bear.

'Now, Corry, we are planning to pick your brains ruthlessly over this dinner, so do come and have a glass of something before we sit down,' Louisa told him, putting her arm through his and leading him towards the sitting room.

'Ho, ho!' cried their jolly guest. 'My poor old brain is yours to pick as you will! A small price to pay for one of *your* dinners, Louisa! But I 'ope you will show me your latest canvases too.'

'Really? You really want to see them? They are just the usual portraits of scholars and dignitaries.'

'Now, now, no false modesty, Louisa, old girl! Of course I want to see 'em. Lead on to the studio immediately!'

The way Corry Long examined Aunt Louisa's work, his handling of the canvases, his close-up scrutiny of the brushstrokes and the colours left Vita in no doubt as to his expertise.

'Fine work! Just as I thought, Louisa. You haven't lost your touch. I only hope the stuffed shirts appreciate 'em. If you need another client, just say the word. I could have crowned heads queuing at your door for a portrait like this.'

Delighted, Aunt Louisa led them to the dining room.

MR CORIOLANUS LONG knew how to do justice to a good dinner. They enjoyed several courses before serious conversation could resume, but over pears poached in wine and served in a chocolate sauce, the strange postcard was introduced at last.

'Show me,' Corry said, wiping his moustache on his napkin and pushing back his chair. He examined the postcard intently by the light of the candles on the table, pulling a small magnifying glass from a pocket and angling the card this way and that. 'Well, I'm blowed,' he declared several times before putting the magnifying glass down and smiling back at the ladies. 'It's a good 'un. I'll say that for it. Fine example, that is. Very nice. Very nice indeed.'

'But what is it, Mr Long? Who would make something like this?' Vita asked.

'Oh, call me Corry, do,' he said. 'Your aunt and I go back a long way. Now, what you 'ave 'ere, as I think you might have guessed, Louisa, is a nice little showpiece. An example of someone's finest work, designed to show off their skills and impress anyone who sees it.'

'It's very clever to paint a stamp, I can see that. And it's well executed, but who would make such a thing?' Vita asked.

Corry paused and looked over at Louisa. 'She's good at asking questions, this young niece of yours, isn't she? Good head on 'er.'

'You can speak freely, Corry, don't worry,' said Louisa, reassuring him.

He nodded. 'Well, in that case, I'll say it's almost certainly a forger's piece. A test piece. I've seen them before. This is a very good one indeed. Do you know the artist?'

'It was found in the room of a young neighbour who died unexpectedly,' Vita told him. 'He was a commercial artist.'

Corry stroked his moustache and frowned. 'I'm sorry to hear he died. I hope he was not a special friend.'

'What do you mean by a forger's piece, Corry?' Vita asked.

Corry took a sip of the port Louisa handed him. 'Well, just between us - your aunt knows this already, of course - I was, in the past, involved in the business of making, shall we say, little *reproductions*. I give it all up now, o' course. Nowadays, Coriolanus Long is the most respectable chap you could 'ope to meet, but long ago, I must admit I turned my hand to a few little copies. It was a natural talent I 'ad, see? I couldn't get money for me own paintings, much as I tried, so I earned a few bob making a copy or two. You know the kind of thing, a Constable-like scene here, a bit of Turner-sort-of landscape there, Gainsborough - I done a few really toothsome Gainsborough portraits in my time. Very popular my Gainsboroughs were.'

He sighed and took a piece of stilton from the cheese board Louisa had placed within reach. 'Galleries commissioned them. They paid me a fair price. If they sold them as originals, it weren't nothing to do with me. I couldn't be held responsible.'

'But you said it was a forger's piece,' Vita said. 'I'm still not quite clear what you meant.'

'She's a proper sharp one, this girl!' Corry said, but he looked pleased as he said it. 'Well, Vita my dear, a forger needs to prove he's good enough, you see. So he makes hisself a little calling card. It might be such a thing as a little Gainsborough miniature, but if it's a different kind of forgery he specialises in - signatures, for an example, or official documents, then he'll make a little something that shows off those skills in particular. So this card, this is telling the would-be customer that the artist in question can fool the Post Office well enough to get a forged stamp franked *and* that he can do a nice signature.'

All three looked closely at the postcard for a moment longer.

'So, the stamp itself isn't really what's important?' asked Aunt Louisa.

'The stamp shows he can make a nice passable working copy of something official, like a stamp, and the signature is a little exhibition of his ability in that department too. The whole thing is a sample to show the quality of a good all-round forger's handiwork.'

'The signature is forged, then?' Aunt Louisa asked.

'Well, that would be my guess. It's a while since I was in the game, meself, as I said. And signatures was never my speciality.'

'Why would Albert Flett post such a thing to himself?'

Corry smiled at them, enjoying his expertise. 'The stamp being franked as genuine by the Post Office demonstrates the high quality of the work. It's a bit of showing off, you might say.'

'So it was Mr Flett's own work?'

'Yes. You said he was an artist.'

'And also a forger, by the look of it.' Vita said.

The term made Corry Long shudder slightly. 'Top notch bit of work, this is. Someone who really knew the game.' Corry Long handed the postcard back to Vita. 'Flett, did you say the fella's name was?'

'Yes. Albert Flett.'

The visitor shrugged, 'I never heard the name, but I can ask around. It's a long while since I was in that game - but I still have friends. Someone might have heard of him. It's small world, the world of *reproductions*.' He gave them a cheery wink as he said the word. 'I'll ask around.'

'You've been invaluable, Corry,' Louisa said, re-filling his glass.

'Anything for you and yours, Louisa, old girl. Anything at all. You only need to ask.'

'HOWEVER DID you meet Mr Long, Aunt?' Vita asked, after their guest had left. Her aunt was locking the front door behind him.

'Oh, I can't remember exactly. One runs across all sorts of interesting people in the art world, Vita,' Louisa said. There was a twinkle in her eye.

It was a poor explanation, Vita thought, as she climbed into bed a little later.

CHAPTER 27

*V*ita was not able to sleep. Her shoulder still ached every time she moved in bed, and she kept thinking of Longbridge's attack in the garden. The power of his arm tightening around her neck had shocked her. Perhaps he would return. Perhaps he was even now climbing the drainpipe.

She told herself to stop being a coward; to get some sleep; to rest so that in the morning she could present a coherent case to Inspector Llewellyn. A case so persuasive that he would be spurred into immediate action and Longbridge would be arrested and taken out of people's gardens for a long time.

But how? Her brain cranked the facts she had collected round like a maid churning butter.

'*Why am I involved anyway?*' she asked herself at about midnight. '*I hardly knew Flett. I cannot really prove that Henrietta Longbridge was killed by her nephew. A feather - is that evidence enough? What does it matter to me, anyhow?*' With a quiet groan at the twinge in her shoulder, she rolled over and tried to empty her mind of the image of the clean soles of Albert Flett's shoes; his neat room; the awful wound in the back of his head.

'*It is the injustice,*' she thought. '*A quiet and kindly young man's life being snuffed out as if nobody cared. As if he didn't really count. That was wrong. But that quiet lodger was also, at least possibly, a forger. That complicates matters, admittedly, but he didn't deserve to die. Nor did Lady Henrietta. Certainly not at the hands of a greedy nephew. And if he has killed twice, why should he hesitate to do so again?*'

By two am, when she heard the hour struck by a distant college chapel bell and repeated by the church at the end of the street, she was asking herself why she, in particular, should involve herself with any of it. '*The police should be solving this crime, not me. I should be reviewing the term's work on the laws of physics, and practising my algebra. And Papa will be here soon and he will ask me if I'm sure, really sure, that all this studying is a good idea. 'You seem to be finding this book work very difficult, Vita,' he'll say. 'Why not come back to the parish? I can find plenty to keep you occupied. You can help me with my notes of bird migrations. We will set up the moth traps in the spring. You already know all the science you need for a good life in Devon, Vita. And you know I would greatly appreciate your help.*'

She reached for the pillow to pull it over her head and muffle these endless thoughts, but as she did so, Vita heard - and she knew exactly what it was from the first second that she heard it - she heard someone unlock the back door. It was Longbridge. She was certain of that too.

She lay for a moment rigid in her bed, holding her breath, focusing every atom of attention on the sound. A muffled scrape - a door opening and closing - he was inside.

Trembling and breathless, Vita crept from her bed, slipped into her dressing gown and stood with her ear to her bedroom door. *What should she do? He might corner her there. He might attack her aunt. He might...*

She caught sight of herself in her dressing table mirror across the room, saw herself tremulous and pale and felt an unexpected surge of something different, something like rage.

I do not have to be afraid of this man! He is in the wrong. He must not be allowed to intimidate me into fearful helplessness. I must not allow it.

Her reflection in the mirror stood taller, breathed more deeply, squared her shoulders; began to formulate a plan. Her bedroom offered few objects that might be useful weapons - an oversight she would remedy in future, she decided - the heaviest things she could see were the textbooks. Grey's Anatomy alone, dropped on a head from above would slow someone down, at the very least, she calculated, and there were several others of equal solidity.

She could shout and wake the house. Tabitha above and her aunt along the landing would soon come running, but would all three of them really be able to stop a determined and desperate young man?

The footsteps were in the hall now, there was no time to lose. She threw open her bedroom door and rushed onto the landing with three of her heaviest books in her arms, and aiming at the point on the staircase she thought most likely, she hurled them over the banister, one after another. They flapped and crashed like heavy birds striking the dark figure on the head, shoulder and back. He cursed loudly and fell to his knees, protecting his head with his arms.

Vita was dashing back to her room to re-arm herself with the next pile of books before she registered the fact that the cursing her bombardment had provoked had been in French.

'*Aieee! Sacrebleu!* Who attacks me?' cried a resentful voice from below.

'Monsieur Picard?' Vita ran back to the banister and leaned over. In the dim staircase she could clearly make out a white haired figure sitting on the stairs. He was rubbing his head and groaning. 'Oh, Monsieur! I thought you were an intruder.'

She had run down by now and was crouching beside the slumped figure. 'Are you hurt?'

'You have attacked me with books! Is this the thanks I receive when I come to see that you and Madame are safe!'

'I can't apologise enough, Monsieur. I heard the door open. I threw the heaviest objects I had in my room.' Vita collected Grey's Anatomy from the foot of the stairs. It seemed unhurt. All the books did. Monsieur's hat, a substantial Homburg which lay beside them, on the other hand, was badly out of shape.

'Alas,' was all he said with a very French shrug when he saw it, 'but it is of less importance than the safety of yourself and Madame, to say nothing of Tabitha. I came to make myself your sentinel, your night watchman. I shall sleep on the sofa with my cleaver.'

'Are you sure?' Vita said.

'Bof!' scoffed Monsieur. 'I am a proud Frenchman. How could I sleep safe in my bed without ensuring that you ladies were defended? You will allow me to perform this small favour, I hope. I shall, perhaps, not see forty again, but I have the heart of a young *chevalier* and my kitchen blades are always perfectly sharp. I have butchered wild boar. A young man of that sort will be no trouble.'

There was no arguing.

'He said he would never see forty again, but his blades were always sharp,' Vita reported to her aunt in the early morning.

'*Forty*?' Louisa said. 'Monsieur will never see *seventy* again, unless I'm much mistaken, but his heart is in the right place. Whatever is that noise?'

They both stopped and leaned toward the bedroom door, open to the landing, before identifying the deep rhythmic sound of the chef's snores vibrating sonorously upstairs from the sofa.

CHAPTER 28

*T*hree cups and saucers had been laid for breakfast when Vita joined her aunt at the table.

'Corry Long is calling round. He wants to keep us informed of his inquiries,' Louisa said.

'That was extremely quick.'

'Corry is not one to let the grass grow under his feet,' her aunt said, 'Any news of the poor cat?'

'Four kittens, all black and white. I peeped. Mother and babies all well.'

'Four! Will you let the professor know? She is his cat, after all.'

'Little Georgie will be delighted, too. I should run and tell him now, perhaps.'

'Stay and see Corry first. The information may be important.'

Corry Long greeted the ladies with his usual Cockney gallantry and was shown into the breakfast room. He turned down the offer of breakfast, but sipped tea and accepted a few biscuits while he explained.

'A good forger - and Albert Flett is considered a good one

by the people I asked - a good forger is a valuable and dangerous commodity. He can change a banker's cheque. He can sign over the deeds of a house; a will; a love letter; an employer's reference. He can do anything. But, really and truly it is the secrets he knows that are valuable. A forger can turn, you see, and use those secrets against his clients.'

'Threaten to reveal the forgery, you mean?' asked Aunt Louisa.

'Exactly so.' Corry leaned back in his chair and gestured with a biscuit in one hand. 'Forgery is a slow and painstaking business; blackmail is quicker and the returns are often better.'

'Albert Flett had money hidden,' Vita said, '£170.'

Long looked surprised at this. 'By rights he should have made a great deal more than that. Either the rest is in the bank, nice and safe, or it's well hidden, or he's been robbed, or he's spent it.'

'He seems to have been a gambler,' Vita said. 'I found a small exercise book which the maid recognised as a form book.'

Corry shook his head. 'My guess would be the daft fella's gone and lost it on the 'orses. He wouldn't be the first. They get drawn in and before they know it, they're in debt and betting some more to try and pay it off. Terrible state of affairs, that is. I seen good men brought to ruin by the gee-gees. Never understood it meself, but it's a kind of bug and once it bites you, it never lets go.' With a look of sorrow he ate two or three more biscuits. 'Did your Frenchman make these? They're proper tasty. Flett's reputation was that of a law-abiding character, was it?'

'Miss Hazelton, his landlady thought him an exemplary character,' Louisa said.

'Well, that's nice. But with all respect to his landlady, it is perfectly possible to lead a double life among well-brought-up and innocent people. They don't know what to look for, you see. The signs could be right there staring them in the face and they'd miss 'em. Albert Flett's reputation among the people I spoke to was this: he was a good forger, sound work, no funny business over his prices; delivered on time. Just what you'd want to see. But he was pressing for more work - big money work. The people I spoke to thought he was impatient. That sort of hastiness can lead to risks.'

'Could that be caused by needing money urgently?' Vita asked.

'It could indeed.'

Aunt Louisa poured their visitor another cup of tea. 'And, Corry, how would a forger usually go about finding extra work, if he needed it?'

Corry smiled. 'Well, for a quick return in Cambridge, the obvious choice is the University men. They run up debts all the time. They don't want Papa and Mamma to know about their indiscretions, so they pay someone like Albert Flett to put the right signature on a banker's cheque on the family account. That's quick work, and not too difficult, for someone who knows his trade. And if the family finds out, they don't hardly ever send the police after the forger. They just want things kept nice and quiet for the reputation of the family, you see.'

'Good heavens!' Aunt Louisa declared. 'What a world you live in, Corry.'

'Not any more, dear lady. All that's in the past for me now,' the gentleman remarked, dusting the crumbs from his moustache,' and very glad I am of it too. Nowadays I just drop into the Fitzwilliam Museum or the National Gallery and they pay me handsomely to look a few canvases over. It's the straight and narrow path for Corry these days!'

Vita said, 'I found a sketchbook hidden. It was strange. It had most of the pages cut out. Neatly removed, but there was one page with the signature *H.B. Longbridge* written several times on one page.'

'He was a tidy worker, you see,' said Corry.

'What do you mean?'

'A forger needs to practice a signature by writing it over and over, but if anyone finds a page of signatures, it's clear proof of what 'e's doing. Your neat forger never keeps the practice pieces. Dear me no! He burns 'em, and he burns 'em quick. I'd guess that poor old Albert Flett met his end before he had the chance to burn that last page.'

'Agnes did say he kept a fire in his grate every night and never carried any waste paper downstairs.'

'He wouldn't, you see. He'd burn the lot. It looks to me as if Flett was a good, careful worker.'

'A good, careful *criminal*,' Louisa remarked.

'Longbridge,' Corry said, after taking a moment to swallow another biscuit, 'Didn't I see that name in the papers?'

'Sadly Lady Henrietta Longbridge died recently, ' Louisa said. 'She was an eccentric local lady and a patron of many charities.'

'Was she now?' Corry said. 'A well-to-do lady, then?' Something in his smile suggested he already knew this. 'I don't wonder you were curious, Miss Carew. You wouldn't happen to have that page of signatures to hand?'

Vita said she had, and hurried to fetch it. When she presented it to Corry, he held it delicately by its edges and looked it minutely over it through the spectacles he kept in his top pocket. 'That is not the signature of a young man. It is the writing of a lady in her seventies, I should say.'

'How can you know that, Corry?' Louisa asked, peering at the paper herself.

'Handwriting is as good as rings in a tree to someone who knows, dear lady. Every generation has its own handwriting. This is the hand of someone who learnt to write more than half a century ago. It is a great deal more formal and intricate - see these flourishes - than you would see in a younger person's hand. This is a gentlewoman's hand, elaborate and slow, the hand of a lady of leisure. A serious, proud, church-going lady, I should say.'

'How can you possibly know that?' Vita asked him.

Corry handed the paper back, smiling. 'It has the flour-ishes of a slow and careful writer who expects people to wait, someone who by nature sticks to what she knows and has no interest in modern ideas.'

Both ladies looked at Corry in amazement, wondering whether he could possibly be serious. He merely smiled.

'I imagine you will take this to the police,' he said.

'Yes, I intend to do so today. So far they have not been much interested in investigating Albert Flett's death, though.'

'Well, watch your step. There's people with a special nose that can sniff a fortune out from several counties away. And they're not very honest people, either. My lips are sealed. I want nothing to do with dodgy dealing, but you ladies had better take care.'

'So wait, let me be clear,' Louisa said, once Corry had been warmly thanked and shown out. 'Albert Flett was a forger of signatures. He probably made a good living at it, but he was short of money sometimes because he gambled on the horse racing.'

'That seems to make sense,' Vita agreed. 'Perhaps he forged a signature or two for Henry Longbridge, and that's how he knew him. Or perhaps they met at the race course.

Anyway, the signature he was practising on the day he died was not *Henry* Longbridge's - at least not according to Corry - it was *Henrietta* Longbridge's. The same aunt who constantly made changes to her will, and who had cut him out as a beneficiary because she detested gambling in all its forms and had discovered her nephew's weakness for the horse racing. Their middle initial must have been the same too.'

'Good heavens! So her nephew might have commissioned Flett to write something in his aunt's handwriting? Such as a codicil to alter her will? And then killed him to keep him quiet?'

'It seems possible,' Vita said.

'And all happening in Eden Street,' her aunt said in wonder, looking out of the window, 'in the house *next door*! This is making me shudder, Vita. You don't think that rude young man who came here the other day could actually have killed his aunt as well, so that he could be sure to benefit from the will before she changed it again?'

'I'm hoping Inspector Llewellyn and his men will decide that, if I can persuade them to take me seriously,' Vita said.

'And meanwhile that same young man is at liberty!'

A loud knock at the front door made them both jump and hold their breath.

'Mr Pottendale to see you, Madam,' Tabitha announced. She was surprised to see the expressions of great relief this brought to the ladies' faces.

'Pottendale! Come to see his portrait. I had completely forgotten,' Louisa said, hurrying to greet him.

· · ·

THE MUSICIAN, who appeared out of breath, managed a shy smile in greeting, but turned to Vita. 'Excuse me. I came, if you will allow it, to alert Miss Carew to something.'

'To what, Mr Pottendale?' asked Vita.

'To an occurrence.'

Both women looked at him expectantly, which made him blink and shift on his feet.

'An occurrence,' he continued, 'at Lady Longbridge's house. *Outside* the house, to be precise.'

'Yes?' Vita tried to urge him in the gentlest way she could manage.

'There is a young gentleman there. Hanging.'

'*Hanging*?' cried both women.

'Yes. I was unlocking the church, as I usually do, and I saw him. At the back of the house. Suspended. I thought you would want to know.'

Vita and her aunt both blinked in alarm, looking first at Pottendale and then, in wonder, at each other.

'Is he ... *dead*?' Vita asked, eventually.

'Dead?' Pottendale looked surprised himself. 'No, no. In fact he is quite lively. Energetic, I would even say. He was wriggling, when I saw him, like an eel on a hook. Upside down. That is why I hurried.'

CHAPTER 29

*A*unt Louisa and Mr Pottendale agreed to search for a police officer, while Vita jumped on her bicycle and pedalled furiously for the Longbridge house and whatever was dangling there.

It was certainly an arresting sight. A man, looking rather like a chrysalis because gravity had turned his jacket inside out and it had fallen over his head, was swinging at the end of a rope tied to a balcony and attached to one ankle. His head was about four feet from the ground. Every now and then, as Vita approached round the side of the building, he squirmed in a great convulsion, very much, she thought, as a chrysalis does just before it hatches. But unlike a moth or butterfly this wriggling creature cursed loudly as it did so.

When he spotted Vita he called, 'Get me down, will you?'

'How did you end up here? What happened?' she said, putting her bicycle against the wall and approaching.

'Never mind that now, just cut this damned rope. I am in severe pain.'

'A police officer will arrive soon.'

'Look, I don't care if the King of England will arrive

175

soon, just get me down. The rope is cutting into my ankle, which is badly sprained. It might be broken. I am in agony.'

'Why are you here? What were you doing? Climbing in? Burgling the house? Don't you have a key?'

'Stop asking questions, damn you! Cut me down!'

'You came for the crowbar,' Vita said.

'Cut this rope. The blood is running to my head. I shall die if I stay this way.'

'That is not very likely,' Vita told him, 'not unless you stayed there for at least a day. Blood doesn't really run to your head when you're upside down. That is a myth.'

'Do you intend to argue with me as I die?'

'Only if you are in the wrong about medical facts,' Vita said. 'Why did you kill Albert Flett?'

'Kill him? I didn't kill him. I don't know what you're talking about.'

'You hit him.'

'I hit him, yes. It was nothing. I didn't kill the man. He fell. I have explained all this to the police. They are perfectly willing to accept it.'

'Why did you hit him?'

'I have told the police. This is nothing to do with you.'

'Was it because he refused to do something you wanted him to do?'

'I have no reason to speak to you about this. Get me down from here, you inquisitive harpy.'

Henry Longbridge twitched on his rope and began to utter a series of coughing, gurgling noises. 'I am feeling faint,' he said, in a wavering tone, 'everything is turning black! The pain! My ankle!'

Vita could see that the ankle knotted in the rope was out of shape. 'It might be broken,' she said, 'you should stay still until help arrives. The police are on their way.'

The hanging man groaned and stopped struggling. The silk lining of his jacket rippled as the wind blew up, shaking the last leaves from the beech tree onto the lawn.

'Did Albert Flett write a new will?'

'What nonsense are you talking now?' he said.

'Your aunt cut you out of her will, didn't she? For gambling?'

The dangling figure was silent. His arms hung limply down over his head. Vita was careful to stand out of range.

'But she changed her will often - everybody in Cambridge knew that - so it was perfectly credible that she might change it back. And if she didn't, Albert Flett would change it for her. Is that right?'

No answer came from the still figure. A crow called from the roof of the church. The rope creaked as it swayed.

Vita stepped a little closer. 'I think you climbed up there and put a pigeon into your aunt's bathroom window. You knew she hated them. You knew it would terrify her. You knew she had a weak heart.'

The dangling figure did not reply, except to groan. Vita leaned towards it. 'I believe you killed your aunt because Albert Flett had forged a codicil to the will and you wanted her dead before she had a chance to make any further changes. You did away with Flett because he might tell.'

The blow, a full-powered uppercut, took Vita off her feet and threw her backwards onto the grass with such force that she thought she might never catch her breath again. Falling, she saw stars and tasted blood, having bitten her own tongue so hard it was four days before she could speak without slurring. But, even as she lay on her back hearing the grunts of rage uttered by the hanging figure, she knew that this violent reaction meant that her accusations must be correct.

. . .

'WHATEVER IS GOING ON HERE?' a cheerful voice demanded. Vita turned her head and saw Adelaide Robinson come round the corner of the house. 'I saw your bicycle. I say, Vita, who's this?'

'It's Henry Longbridge,' Vita said, her speech muffled by pain and a swelling tongue.

'And has this jackanapes just hit you, Vita?' Adelaide asked.

Vita indicated vigorously that he had.

'He seems to have fallen from the balcony, silly boy,' said Adelaide, stepping back to take in the scene. 'He clearly caught his foot in the rope. Schoolboy error. Not the sort of thing a decent night climber should be doing at all. Better than pitching head first over the balcony onto the rockery without one, though.'

Henry Longbridge groaned.

'We should cut him down,' Vita said.

'Isn't he better hanging until the police arrive? You've sent for them, I imagine.'

'Yes. He may be losing consciousness.'

'Is that a problem?'

'It might be. He could die,' Vita told her, brushing blood from her mouth with the back of her hand. 'And we don't want the blood to *wrush* to his head and kill him, we want him to face the *consekuwenshes* of all he has done.' Speech was becoming more difficult by the minute.

'You said it was a myth about blood rushing to the head,' mumbled the hanging man.

'It is, I think, but I'm not *asholutely* sure,'

'Righto,' Adelaide said. 'I have a pocket knife. I'll shin up and cut him down. We don't want him running off, though. There's a rope on my bike. We can truss him securely before we do that, just to be on the safe side. The trick will be to avoid another punch from the coward.'

'Is that *poshible*?' Vita asked, nursing her sore face.

Adelaide shrugged. 'I've roped calves before now,' she said. 'I imagine I can lasso his hands from a safe distance. Once they're secure we can just tie him up like a big joint of pork.'

Longbridge uttered a stream of terrible oaths. He squirmed, swung, flailed, and generally resisted with all his might, growing redder and more enraged with every curse, but eventually Adelaide's plan worked.

By the time the police arrived, their suspect was a foul-mouthed but otherwise helpless tweed bundle, pinned face down on the grass by two young women sitting on his back.

'I'm sure there's someone in the house,' Vita said, after Long-bridge had been taken away by the police officers. The two young women had wheeled their cycles to the front, ready to leave. Vita looked back at Langcragg's shuttered windows. 'I had a feeling we were being watched earlier, and the window was opened the time before, when we were on the balcony, remember.'

'Yes, I do,' Adelaide said. 'Shall we knock?'

Vita nodded. They leaned their bicycles against the building again and knocked on the great front door. The immense door knocker was in the shape of a dragon.

Nothing happened for several minutes, but then slow footsteps approached from inside and an elderly manservant in black slowly opened the door by six inches. He was a tall man with a beak-like nose and heavy white eyebrows.

'You were employed by Lady Longbridge, I think?' Vita asked. 'Your name is Timpson?'

He did not reply, but only looked at Vita with haughty suspicion.

'I saw you pushing her chair once. At the solicitors.'

This also brought no response for several minutes, before he said, 'My wife and I have spoken at length to the police.' Vita could see another figure, presumably his wife, approaching behind him. He began to close the door.

Vita leaned forward and spoke through the narrowing gap between the heavy door and its frame. 'Mr Timpson, I believe that Henry Longbridge is implicated in Lady Longbridge's death,' she said. The door closed abruptly on that last word. She continued to address the man behind it, raising her voice to be heard. 'He is a ruthless man, Mr Timpson, you and your wife should be very concerned for your own safety, especially if he has promised you money when he does inherit.'

No answer came, except the hurried sliding of bolts behind the door.

As Vita and Adelaide turned to leave, they heard voices inside the house begin an urgent conversation.

CHAPTER 30

here was a definite aroma of toasted teacake that afternoon in Inspector Llewellyn's office. Constable White was ready at his desk in the corner to take notes. The Inspector, dashing the odd crumb from his beard, was in an expansive and benign frame of mind.

'This won't take long, Miss Carew. Clarification is needed on one or two details, that is all.' Constable White's pencil scratched in the corner. 'We know most of the facts in this case now. Are these the items you found in Flett's room?'

'Yes. The postcard, the racing form book and the sketchbook.'

'Indeed,' Llewelyn said, glancing without much interest at the objects before him on the desk. 'And from these you deduced what?'

'That Albert Flett was a forger, and an able one, but that he was also a gambler.'

'Quite the little detective, aren't we? Quite the lady Sherlock Holmes! If I had a shilling for every clever University man or woman who thought they could outmanoeuvre the dull old police force, I should be as rich as the late Lady Longbridge.'

Llewellyn chucked and glanced over at his constable, but White was too hunched over his writing to appreciate his Inspector's wit.

'There was a bruise on Albert Flett's chin. He had been punched,' Vita said.

'Yes. Longbridge has confessed to hitting him. Flett owed him money. He refused to pay. Longbridge punched him. The fall and the injury were accidental and Flett's skull was thin. All this is confirmed by the police surgeon. Flett was unlucky. There is no evidence for murder.'

Llewellyn drummed his fingers briefly on his blotter. 'It was quick-witted of you to identify Longbridge as the man who had called on Flett, and to work out that someone must have hidden in the roof, I admit. But still, none of this amounts to anything more than circumstantial detail. We in the police force must abide by the requirements of the law, you see.'

The bruise had been on Vita's jaw for long enough to spread and grow darker. A high-necked blouse, intended to conceal at least part of the purple blot, merely acted as contrast and made it stand out more. Her neck was stiff and her tongue still swollen, her speech slow and humiliatingly indistinct.

'Neighbours saw Henry Longbridge on the outside of his aunt's house the night she died,' Vita said, struggling with the pronunciation of the name Longbridge, in particular. It came out as *Longvwishe*, however much she tried. 'There were witnesses.'

'None of them was able to identify him. They saw something, but it might have been anyone.'

'He is a night climber. It is his aunt's house. He wanted to inherit.'

'All true enough, but circumstantial, as I have explained. I'm sorry Miss Carew, but you have let your ideas run away with you. I suggest you set all these thoughts aside from now on, and return to your other interests. Scientific matters, I believe you are devoted to, or some such.'

'And *Longvwishe*?' Vita asked, pressing her hand to her jaw to ease the pain of saying the troublesome name out loud.

'We cannot lay charges against a gentleman just because someone *fancies* he has committed a crime. The streets would be empty, if we did that!'

'But he had climbed up to reach a crowbar that has his fingerprints on it.'

'Fingerprints!' said Llewellyn rolling his eyes. 'You have been reading the Police Gazette again. Fingerprints, indeed.'

The Inspector enjoyed his quip, checking that PC White appreciated it as well, but the constable still avoided his eye.

'Miss Carew, the man you and your friend tied up is the future owner of that house. If he chooses to break into it with or without a crowbar, it is nobody's business but his own.'

'He has assaulted me on more than one occasion,' Vita said.

'He denies that. He has never been in your back garden, and he claims the most recent episode - I can see it was quite a blow - was entirely accidental. He was unable to see. He hit out when someone threatened him. He was in pain. His ankle was badly sprained. He has apologised.'

'What makes you defend him? Why do you take his side?'

'I have explained before. Innocent until proved guilty. You are free to press assault charges. I you have witnesses, the case will be proved.'

'I have no witnesses.'

'Exactly.' Llewellyn placed his hand on the papers she had brought. 'And what you have in this dossier, as far as I can see, is a long list of very neatly written details amounting to nothing that would be useful in a court case. It has no doubt amused you to write this, but it is of no use to the police force.'

'You haven't even read it!'

'I shall ask an officer to take a look. Constable White here, for example. I am a busy man. Miss Carew is leaving, Constable. You can show her downstairs.'

'WHY?' Vita asked White on the stairs. 'Why won't he act?'

'We can't go arresting university gentlemen - people with titles, or soon to have titles - people like Longbridge - without all the proper evidence. They have powerful connections. The Chief Constable for one,' White said.

'But Longbridge is so obviously…'

Another policeman appeared in the hall and began to climb the stairs. No more could be said.

A NOTE HAD BEEN DELIVERED by the university mail service while Vita was at the police station. Pulling off her hat and coat in the hall at Eden Street, she recognised the handwriting of her college tutor immediately.

'You look alarmed, dear,' Aunt Louisa remarked, when she saw her.

'It is a note from Miss Ledbetter,' Vita said, 'I expect she wants to see me.'

'You might open it, just to be sure.'

'I dread it,' Vita said.

'Is she such a dragon, this Miss Ledbetter?'

Vita continued to stare miserably at the envelope. 'It's worse than that. She is calm and kind, but she is also the one who will decide my future at the college. Whether or not I have a future, that is.'

'Do you seriously doubt that? Oh my word, whatever has happened to your face? I thought you were at the police station.'

Without answering, Vita opened the envelope and read the note. '*Please call at four o'clock this afternoon,*' she read aloud, '*to discuss reports and evaluate the term's progress.*'

'Ah,' said her aunt, 'I was about to tell you that four o'clock is exactly the time your father is due to arrive. You will miss his arrival, but not to worry, you will have news from college when you do see him. At least you have a few hours to put a cold compress on that dreadful bruise before you go.'

'Ish my tongue thash the real problem,' Vita said.

'Ice. I shall send Tabitha to fetch some ice. And meanwhile you should ask Dr Goodman to examine it when you go to tell George that Minmou is safe. Tabitha offered to tell him about the kittens, but I thought it would be better coming from you, dear.'

LITTLE GEORGIE ABSORBED the news with wide-eyed amazement. He sat on the stairs in silence for a moment, and then jumped off the third step to celebrate before galloping upstairs shouting, 'Kittens! Baby kittens! Minmou has kittens!'

Out of sight upstairs a stampede of running footsteps could be heard and then simultaneous shrieks of delight from his four sisters as the news spread. These continued for several minutes, but then a hush fell, and a door closed above.

Their mother, standing in the hall with Vita, sighed. 'Oh dear, I thought that would happen,' she said. 'They know better than to rush immediately and ask if they can have a kitten. Their father has steadfastly refused all ideas of puppies and kittens in the past. He says he has enough mouths to feed in this household already. So now my children are no doubt developing a detailed and subtle campaign of action, designed to change his mind.'

'And are you against the idea yourself, Mrs Goodman?' Vita asked.

'I had better maintain a neutral stance, I think,' the children's mother said. 'Are they all black and white, did you say?'

CHAPTER 31

*C*ambridge cyclists are generally agreed that a ride to Newton College is always uphill against a strong headwind in both directions. That afternoon, three separate brief but penetrating showers of rain also soaked Vita on the fifteen minute journey. To someone on the way to a much-feared meeting, it felt like one ill omen after another. She arrived at Miss Ledbetter's study with her hat out of shape, her glasses steamed up, and her coat and boots drenched. Add to this the bruise on her jaw and the graze on her nose, and the undergraduate facing her Senior Tutor presented a pitiful sight.

Miss Ledbetter was of the school of etiquette that never stooped to remark on anyone's personal appearance.

'Thank you for coming at short notice, Miss Carew,' she said, looking at her wristwatch. 'We will begin immediately, if you don't mind, as I have a meeting at half past. Please sit down. Now,' she glanced at the papers on her desk, 'we must, I think, take a straightforward and practical approach to the situation at hand. You have recently sat one of your papers - anatomy was it?'

'Yes,' Vita said, gloomily.

'The professor insists that Anatomy is taken early, does he?'

'Yes.'

'And you have the result?'

'No.'

'It was not posted outside the Senate House, as usual?'

'No. I looked.'

Miss Ledbetter frowned. 'A late result is generally not a good sign. I think we should assume the worst. Unless you are particularly optimistic about the result?'

'No.'

'Ah. Pessimistic, I see.' A note was added to the papers.

'Your other reports are mixed, this term. Maths, Physics and Chemistry seem to have been difficult, as well as Anatomy. Would that be correct?'

'Yes,' Vita said. Her own monosyllabic answers were beginning to irritate her.

Miss Ledbetter set the papers aside and looked up at her battered and damp student. 'Miss Carew, there comes a point - I say this to many students - there comes a point where the strain of attempting to keep up with a course of study is simply too much. Do you understand? A losing battle.'

Vita nodded, looking at the carpet.

'This is no judgement upon you personally. It is a Herculean task to learn all the principles of science you need in a single year. We have long argued, here at Newton, that at least two years of academic preparation are needed for many young women to put them on anything like an equal footing with young men from good schools.'

Vita could only nod at the floor again.

'I always tell undergraduates that nothing is gained by making a rod for your own back. There are other subjects besides science. Or you might consider intermitting for a year, taking some intensive tutoring and returning when you are better equipped. Year upon year of punishing failure is no good for anyone. I have seen young women's spirits broken by it, with terrible consequences in some cases.'

Vita could not bring herself to look up. 'Will you recommend that I leave the college?'

Miss Ledbetter looked away, out of the window, where a grey rain was falling on the gardens at a steady forty-five degree angle. A coal shifted in the fireplace. 'It has not come to that yet,' she said. 'What I would recommend is that you re-examine your choice of subject. Consider finding a course of study more suited to your current level of learning, and your personal inclination. I hear, for example, that you speak a number of languages. You might consider transferring to Modern Languages. Will you at least contemplate that?'

Vita shook her head, 'I have only ever wanted to study Medicine. This was my only hope of doing so. My father was reluc…*reluctant.*' She struggled to pronounce the word, her tongue still painful. 'I had hoped in this year to convince him I was capable. Funds are limited.'

'That is often the case, I'm afraid,' Miss Ledbetter said, looking again at her watch. 'Come and see me again in a week. There is no shame in attempting something extremely difficult, falling short, and adjusting one's ambitions to something more attainable. No shame at all. Bear that in mind.'

She stood and began gathering papers. 'Now, if you will forgive me, I must go. We shall speak again next week. By all means, stay here by the fire and warm yourself.'

Miss Ledbetter swept out of the room, closing the double doors behind her, leaving Vita in silence to stare into the fire and picture her ambitions turning to dust and ashes just as the coals were.

~

AUNT LOUISA HAD none of Miss Ledbetter's restraint when it came to Vita's appearance, greeting her with exclamations of horror on her return.

'Vita! You'll catch pneumonia! You must change your clothes immediately!'

'Your aunt is right, my dear child, you put your health at great risk going about in that state. Go and change into something warm and dry.'

After the briefest of greetings to her father, Vita did as she was told. Her father and aunt watched the bedraggled figure hurry up the stairs.

'I have always said that the climate in Cambridge is a pernicious one, Louisa, have I not? It is the merciless flatness of the landscape. It is notoriously malarial, you know. The country people in these parts are famous for their ill-health.'

'Perhaps that is so in the remote fens, Stephen,' Louisa said, taking her brother's arm, 'but half my neighbours here in Eden Street are over eighty, so it does not hold true in the city.' She guided her brother back to the fireside.

The Reverend Stephen Carew was a little taller than his sister. They were close in age, but his white hair and weather-beaten complexion made him look much older. He wore black from head to toe except for his white clerical collar. He shared his sister's bright blue eyes, but where Louisa's often shone with natural merriment, there was a cast of seriousness, and a darting anxiety - to her brother's look.

'You will understand my concern about the child, Louisa. She seems from her letters always to be rushing, always in a flurry of pressure and nervous anxiety. It is not natural in one so young.'

'Really, Stephen, Vita is preoccupied at present, I admit,

but in general she is thriving under the challenge of her studies.'

'And whatever happened to her face? She looks as if she had been in the boxing ring.'

'A bruise, merely. Nothing of concern.'

'She fell off that bicycle of hers, no doubt. I have had my reservations about that contraption from the very start.'

Louisa made herself busy with the fire. It seemed wiser to avoid telling her brother that Vita had been punched by a murder suspect.

Reverend Carew took an armchair and stretched out his hands to warm them. 'I gave my consent for Victoria to test herself in the academic world. I believed - I would even say I hoped - that it would serve to disillusion her. A young woman of little experience is likely to glorify the unattainable. She has always been an inquisitive girl, but that is not the same as having academic ability to any serious level.'

'She had hardly any schooling, Stephen, as you know. It set her at a disadvantage.'

'She nursed her mother. It was a duty she embraced willingly, and she did it well.'

'Indeed. Her brother, of course, was free to go to school.'

'A young man must have an education. This is not too old-fashioned an idea, surely?'

'Not at all, no.' Louisa took the chair across the fireplace from her brother. She reached across and patted his hand. 'Stephen, I have enjoyed having Vita here with me, and I have learnt a great deal about her. I was speaking only recently to one of her tutors. I'm told that academically she has exceptional potential.'

'Exceptional? How so? She seems to me a dutiful enough girl, and obedient, most of the time, but not outstanding, intellectually speaking.'

'I am no judge of that, but what I have seen is a truly impressive combination of practical thinking, diligent study and extraordinary dedication. I am no expert, but these seem to me ideal qualities in a medical practitioner.'

'A medical practitioner?' Stephen Carew raised his eyebrows. 'The best she could hope for is some role in nursing - dirty, unappealing work - or a clinic for the poor somewhere. I cannot see how that is preferable to a healthy life in the country. Plenty of my parishioners need the kind of medical help that she could provide already, without years of study and examinations. She might marry a medical man, I suppose, but the wife of a country doctor has little to recommend it.'

'I only urge you to listen to her, Stephen. Allow her to put her own case.'

The vicar sighed and shook his head. 'What good would it do to encourage her? You know there are insufficient funds to support her studies. Her mother's money is almost exhausted. The bursary the college granted lasts only until May. You would not have me bankrupt myself, I presume.'

'Of course not. But you will allow her to put her point of view?'

'I am not a tyrant, Louisa, I will, of course, listen to what she has to say. I realise I have been guilty in the past of taking my daughter for granted. I did perhaps lean on her too much during her mother's last illness. I consented to her following her brother to Cambridge. I had no expectation of her embarking on a course of study of any great length or complexity. Why should she? She will remember her time at Newton College for the rest of her days in Devon, I'm sure. Education is never wasted, even if it has to be curtailed.'

CHAPTER 32

*V*ita, having changed her clothes, paused at the top of the stairs, steeling herself for the meeting with her father. She dreading the inevitable discussion. Her feet were unwilling to take the next step down, but were jolted into action by appearance in the hall of Tabitha with a tea tray. The maid looked relieved to see Vita.

'Miss, could you spare a minute? Only Agnes Venner's at the back door and she's all a-quiver. I can't get her to come in. She's asking for you. It must be you, she says. I told her you had a visitor, but she won't take no for an answer.'

VITA URGED Agnes into the kitchen and sat her at the table. The maid was wringing her hands. 'I had to come, Miss. I should have told you before. I was so worried about the *money,*' the word was whispered behind her hand, 'that it went out of my poor head. I swear it did.'

'What did?'

Agnes looked at her wide-eyed. 'The letter,' she finally said.

'Which letter is that?'

'This one,' Agnes said. 'It was there in the hiding place under the floorboards with the... *money*. I put it in my apron pocket and forgot all about it until I found it just now. What shall I do with it, Miss?'

Vita took the sealed envelope from Agnes's shaking hand. It was inscribed in an artistic script with the words *To be opened in the event of my sudden death*. The stamp, an ordinary red one penny stamp, had, upon examination, been painted.

The envelope, still sealed, remained on her desk throughout Vita's discussion with her father, the awkward dinner that followed, and the evening cut short both by his tiredness and Vita's feelings of bleak hopelessness about her future studies.

She only remembered it when she slumped into the chair in her bedroom, and saw it again, propped against the beautiful illustration of the hand and wrist in her open copy of Grey's Anatomy.

She opened the envelope and read.

To whom it may concern,

I, the undersigned, wish it to be known that Mr Henry Longbridge of Pembroke College befriended me at a race-track. We became (as I then thought) friends, and often went to dog and horse racing meetings in each other's company. I later learnt that when we first met, he already knew my reputation as someone who was able occasionally to offer my artistic services to gentlemen in difficulties, but I did not know then. Not long after we met, he asked me to put his aunt's signature to a letter of credit. My income at that time being uncertain due to a run of ill luck, I accepted the commission in return for a payment of three guineas.

Longbridge visited me several times more on the same errand. In June this year he asked me to place bets for him with his bookmaker, as his aunt had tyrannically forbidden his attendance at Newmarket or any other racecourse. I performed this service then, and on many occasions thereafter. I should like it noted that Mr Longbridge, in that time, made a substantial loss. He enjoys gambling, but has no talent for it, and never listened to my advice.

In September this year Longbridge asked me to write a codicil letter in the hand of his aunt, altering her will in his favour. He said he was in debt and desperate, and that the old lady was cruelly changeable in the details of his inheritance, causing him suffering and doubt as to his future. He said he wanted only to secure what was rightfully his due.

I refused this commission but Longbridge would not accept my refusal. He made the same demand on three or four further occasions, threatening me with violence. I began to fear for my own safety. Two weeks ago, having hit another run of bad luck, I gave in and did as he asked. I charged him 20 guineas, which he has yet to pay.

I immediately regretted my decision to write this codicil. Henry Longbridge now has a strong incentive to procure the death of his aunt in order to obtain his inheritance. I believe him more than capable of doing this and he has, on several occasions, mentioned the possibility of doing so. I am also increasingly certain that he plans to end my life in order to preserve this secret.

If this letter is found, my money will also have been found. I have no heirs. If an honest person finds this letter and my savings, I should like the money to be given to my landlady, Miss Hazelton, and her maid, Agnes Venner. Both have treated me more kindly than I deserve.

I have made poor use of my talents. May God forgive me.

In sorrow,
Albert Flett

CHAPTER 33

*L*lewellyn read the letter frowning through the reading glasses on the end of his nose. 'You found this where, did you say?'

'In a hiding place under the floorboards of Albert Flett's room.'

'You found it yourself?'

'The maid found it.'

'And how do we know it was genuinely written by Mr Flett?'

'By the stamp.'

Llewellyn raised one eyebrow and squinted at the stamp. 'Looks like an ordinary penny stamp to me,' he said.

'Yes, but it's not a real stamp. It is the painting of a stamp. It is Flett's trademark. It is unique to him.'

The Inspector looked skeptical. He laid the envelope on his desk and peered at it, then ran an index finger across. 'My word! You're right. It isn't there at all. It's just painted on. Come and have a look at this, Constable White. Did you ever see the like? It's cleverly done, I'll say that for it. Mind you, it's a serious offence, forging a stamp.'

'Mr Flett doesn't need to worry about that any more,' Vita reminded him.

'The letter makes very serious allegations. I am not sure how much weight it would carry as evidence,' Llewellyn remarked, still peering at the stamp.

Vita felt her patience drain away. She suddenly felt tired to her bones. 'It matches the stamp on the postcard I found in Flett's room. The postcard and the sketchbook both show that Flett was capable of forging Lady Longbridge's signature. Who would benefit from such a forgery but the nephew she had cut out of her will for gambling? Is there absolutely nothing that will persuade you that Henry Longbridge, even if he is, on the face of it, a gentleman and a scholar, is also a murderer?'

She stood to leave. 'You will understand, Inspector, that I might feel irritated at the idea of Longbridge lying comfortably in his rooms at Pembroke College when he has killed two people! And of course he may not be in his rooms, he could even now be on the way to the Continent or boarding a ship for America!'

'As a matter of fact, Miss Carew, he is in the cells downstairs,' Llewellyn said. 'There was a significant development in our investigations last night. I carried out the arrest myself at about eight o'clock. Mr Longbridge had just finished dinner. I suspect that will be the last college dinner - guinea fowl, I believe it was - that he will be eating for quite some time.'

The Inspector sat back in his chair with an air of satisfaction. The rows of police officers in the long photographs on the wall behind him all seemed to stare smugly back at Vita as well.

'May I ask what the significant development was?' she asked.

'No, Miss Carew, you may not,' said the Inspector. 'This letter will be of some small secondary use as evidence, together with what you call your *dossier*,' he chuckled at the word. 'But it is honest police work that has solved this case. You have done your duty now. My constable will show you out.'

Constable White followed Vita down the flight of stairs from Llewellyn's office. As he did so, he coughed slightly twice, and on each occasion she thought she heard him say the name 'Timpson' under his breath. When she looked over her shoulder, the young constable's face was a perfectly innocent blank.

A FIGURE she recognised was just ahead of Vita as she left the police station. It was Marcus Waring.

'What brings you to the police station, Miss Carew?' he asked pleasantly when he saw her.

'Nothing of any importance. At least, Inspector Llewellyn doesn't think so,' she said.

'He's made an arrest in the Longbridge case,' Waring said. 'I expect he's preoccupied with that.'

'He told me. The nephew.'

'It is a tragic state of affairs,' Waring said. 'Betrayed by her nephew and her most long serving servant. He'd been with her for over thirty years.'

'Would that be Timpson?'

'Yes. I've just witnessed his statement. It'll all be out in public soon. Poor man put up with years of poor treatment from Lady Longbridge. She cut him out of her will and put him back two or three times, to my knowledge. He shouldn't have agreed to any plan Henry Longbridge suggested, but you can see why he might be tempted.'

'Timpson agreed to murder her?'

'No, nothing like that. The man's nearly seventy. He simply agreed to go out for the evening when Longbridge asked him.'

'Did he know why Longbridge asked him to do so?'

'Longbridge promised him ten guineas. A huge sum to a manservant. He asked no questions.'

'Will he hang?'

'Timpson? I doubt it. He is an accessory, no more.'

'And Henry Longbridge?'

'On two counts of murder? If they are proven, he will certainly hang.' They walked a few paces further. 'Does that please you, Miss Carew? A satisfactory outcome, perhaps?'

'Satisfactory? A hanging could never be satisfactory,' Vita said. The cold seemed suddenly to pierce her clothing. She shivered.

'I doubt it will come to that. A good lawyer would dispute much of the evidence,' Waring continued. 'The case will be heard in Bedford, I imagine, or London. They won't hold it in Cambridge, where all possible jurors will have feasted on every detail of the case in the newspapers. It's a notorious case. Some young barrister will use it to found a career.'

He turned to Vita and raised his hat. 'And that is why I have a practice in wills and conveyancing. The less dramatic legal activities are far more to my taste. The Amateur Musical Society's next Gilbert and Sullivan can be my preoccupation, rather than keeping my clients from the hangman's noose. Good day, Miss Carew. My mother would wish me to thank you again. Her hand is almost healed.'

CHAPTER 34

'*Y*our father and I thought we might make a little outing to Ely today, Vita,' Louisa said when she returned from the police station. 'It is a long time since either of us saw the cathedral, and we can take luncheon at The Lamb. You would be welcome to join us.'

It was the last thing Vita felt like doing. To judge from his expression, the trip had not been her father's idea either. But Louisa was not to be stopped.

'Come, Stephen, it will do you good. There is nothing like the beauty and grandeur of a cathedral to drive away the tribulations of day-to-day life and put matters into perspective, besides, Mr Pottendale is giving a lunchtime recital.'

'I am well aware of the merits of cathedrals already,' her brother said. 'And who is this Pottendale character?'

'He is the first of many portrait commissions from Trinity College, I rather hope,' Louisa said, 'and also an expert organist. *Toccata and Fugue in D minor* on the Ely cathedral organ. It should be most impressive! If we leave now, we can catch the train at ten past eleven. Come along now, Stephen dear, this is a spectacle you will not find in your parish in Devon!'

WHEN VITA VISITED the usual noticeboard outside the Senate House for the second time, the anatomy results had finally been posted, but although she peered with and without her spectacles, her name did not appear anywhere on the list. In increasing dismay, she read the results for every other examination taken that term - from Hebrew II to Geology IV, running her finger down the handwritten lists, but found no V. Carew on any of them.

Dr Underhill's brief summons was at Eden Street when she returned. Perhaps he wanted to explain in person why she had been left off the list altogether. *It was not worth putting your name so low on the list. It was not fit to be listed in any way*, Vita's gloomy imagination had him declare. *It is the worst examination result we have ever experienced in the anatomy department, so we decided to erase it from history.*

She was early, but couldn't settle to anything else, so she walked instead of cycling, pausing to look into shop windows and read notices along the way, making the walk as slow as possible, like someone on their way to the gallows.

The Police Surgeon's office was in the laboratory building, along the corridor from the post mortem theatre. It was tucked away and difficult to find. When Vita finally located the door with the sign 'Police Surgeon, please knock and enter', she was surprised at how small and crowded it was. A desk in a corner was overshadowed by row upon row of biological specimens in labelled jars lining one wall and books lining the others. An inner door was open showing a glimpse of a large room filled with empty dissecting tables. The bearded post mortem technician Vita had seen at work before was moving about, apparently cleaning and tidying equipment.

'Ah, Miss Carew,' Underhill had followed her in. 'Thank you for coming. Perhaps we should talk in the post mortem theatre, there is more room. This way.'

Underhill led her through the inner door and past the dissecting tables. The technician looked gravely up and nodded. Another door and they were in the empty and echoey space of the theatre, surrounded by the raked wooden seats.

Across the room, Vita could see the door she had caught her skirt in, and had a moment to re-live that humiliation.

Underhill gestured her to sit on a bench in the front row. He stayed in the centre, pacing slightly, which might have seemed odd to Vita if she hadn't been too anxious to think anything other than gloomy thoughts of failure and despair.

'So,' he said. 'It seems we have an acquaintance in common. You were a pupil of Emily Shorto's, I believe.'

'Yes. Miss Shorto was my first teacher of anatomy, and science in general, in fact. I was very sorry when she went away.'

'You know that she has returned?'

'No! I did not know.'

'Only quite recently.' Underhill had stopped pacing. A distinctly merry look had come into his eyes. He bent forward and directed a smile at his toecaps, as if trying to control it. 'She left her mother in Chile to continue her collecting, but chose to return to Cambridge herself.'

Vita nodded politely.

'Her mother is a very distinguished botanist, as I'm sure you know,' Underhill went on, 'but Emily - Miss Shorto, that is, has her own work to pursue in Huntingdon Road. She intends to resume teaching as well.'

'That is good news,' Vita said, sadly. She could not feel this had anything to do with her own bleak future.

'The fact is,' Dr Underhill said, resuming his up and down pacing, 'that Miss Shorto and I have discussed your case at some length. I have known her well for many years. Emily - Miss Shorto - has made strong representations on your behalf. Very strong. I am - perhaps you know this - not, strictly speaking, part of the University. I am employed by the Constabulary, but I do some some teaching, and examining and instructing in post mortem technique, anatomy and so forth.' He waved his arms as he walked. Something about the mention of Miss Shorto made him accelerate his pace.

Vita had no idea where this was leading. She could only watch, her knuckles whitening as she clung to the narrow wooden shelf that acted as a desk in front of the seat.

Underhill returned from another of his circuits. 'We are both of the opinion that your work is promising, but that at this stage you are not performing particularly well, academically speaking. Would you agree with this?'

'I would, I'm afraid.'

'What you need - incidentally, I discussed this with your tutor, Miss Ledbetter this morning - what you need is a period of intensive revision. Am I correct?'

'Yes, but there is a difficulty…'

'… with funds? Yes, I'm coming to that.' He walked away again, but this time only as far as a high stool near the post mortem table in the centre of the theatre, where he perched, a hand on each knee. 'Miss Shorto is willing to offer your tuition at a reduced rate, and in order to help pay for that, and your other college fees, I intend to offer you a post here as a post mortem assistant. The payment is not large, but the work is steady and you will, of course, learn a great deal.

It is a few hours a week, but, if you prove apt, it will be time well spent, even if it is very early in your medical training.'

Vita looked back in stunned silence, so Underhill went on.

'Miss Ledbetter has agreed this plan. What do you make of it?'

'A paid role? Here? In the post mortem theatre?'

'Here, yes, and wherever else you may be needed.'

He stood, ready to leave.

'And Miss Ledbetter agreed?' Vita asked, still trying to make sense of what she had heard.

'She did. I'll leave you to consider. Send a note when you have made a decision. And if you accept the position, I shall start your training on Monday next.'

'Why? Why are you offering this to me? There are so many other students. Did I even pass the anatomy test? My name was not even on the list.'

'Your name was third on the list. I have a copy on my desk.'

'But I looked! I couldn't see it!'

He waved this aside as foolishness. 'Emily - Miss Shorto, I should say is convinced you have the makings of a fine medic. The little I have seen of your reaction to post mortem work has certainly been encouraging.'

'I was in a cupboard!'

'You found a way. Most students merely tolerate this work; you seem to have a natural inclination towards it. That is rare.'

'Thank you,' was all Vita could manage to say.

Underhill turned for the door. 'I need no thanks,' he said. 'I need hard work. And, Miss Carew, *be on time.*'

CHAPTER 35

*I*f Vita had brought her bicycle, she would probably have rushed home on it, but as she was on foot, and the day was clear and bright, she walked in the direction of the Backs to give herself time to think about Dr Underhill's extraordinary offer. A paid role. A minor role, and no sum of money had been mentioned, but an official role working on post mortems with the Police Surgeon. She wondered if she would be up to it. She wondered what it would entail. She wondered if she would have to show herself in public, or be hidden in the back room (which might be better). Perhaps she would mostly be cleaning? (She didn't care.) Perhaps she would be asked to do things she didn't understand. Perhaps...

At this point in her deliberations she collided at speed with another pedestrian on Silver Street bridge.

PC White had also been lost in thought, but his speculations had been about whether he would be picked for Cambridge Police's rugby first team. He had the flushed cheeks of one who had played a vital part in the winning try ten minutes before – a fifty-yard dash, head down, through a crowd of defenders. But that was in practice. He hoped he had not peaked too soon and could reproduce the dash, or even improve on it, against Huntingdon Constabulary's first XV to clinch the local derby on Saturday. They would cheer him to the rafters. They would pay for his beer all night long.

'Oh! I do beg your pardon!'

The young woman he had charged into looked apologetic herself. 'I should have been looking! I have dropped my spectacles. They must be nearby. Can you see them?'

Vita looked about, but White had already spotted the glasses and retrieved them from the pavement. He handed them to her, and she twisted the frame a little and put them on again. 'It is you, Constable White. I did not recognise you. I hope you are not hurt. I was miles away.'

'I was too.'

They smiled at one another for a moment. Out of uniform, Constable White seemed taller, she thought, more freckled and less starchy. He was carrying a boot bag.

'I must cut along, I am on duty in twenty minutes,' he said.

'There was something I wanted to ask. May I accompany you?'

'Of course, but, Miss Carew, I hope you will not be asking for information about any current investigations. I am not permitted to answer that sort of question.'

'I want to know why Llewellyn changed his mind and arrested Henry Longbridge,' Vita said. They walked together towards St Botolph's church.

'That is precisely the kind of question I cannot answer. It would be most improper.'

'I told him all sorts of information about Longbridge, but he did nothing. Then all of a sudden...'

'As I said, I cannot discuss that.'

'Everything will be declared in open court quite soon, surely?'

'That does not mean it is public knowledge now,' White said, sternly.

'I have wracked my brains. I made allegations, but not enough to prompt Llewellyn into action. So what did?'

They were close to King's College now, heading for Great St Mary's. The clock struck the quarter hour. White picked up the pace. He still said nothing, but his face wore a calm and slightly playful expression.

Vita continued, lengthening her pace to keep up. 'My guess is that he would interview character referees in a case like Longbridge's. Probably a friend or two and - well, I would imagine someone from his college. A senior tutor?'

White, still smiling faintly, walked towards the market.

'You would have been there to take notes. That is your role, to be in the Inspector's office, taking verbatim notes.'

He kept walking.

'So you would have been present if they came to the police station. And if he visited witnesses, you would have gone with him.'

Their pace was slowed by crowds of shoppers in the market. Stalls selling fish and meat as well as china, clothing, vegetables and books were doing brisk trade on both sides.

'I imagine he interviewed some fellow students. It would have been easy for Longbridge to persuade friends to vouch for him. A betting man who liked a drink, he would have plenty of college friends. He chose the titled ones to speak to Llewellyn, I imagine. Lord this and Lord that. And they all said he was a fine fellow. Sound as a bell. Am I right?'

White did not reply, but continued to pick his way across

the cobblestones in the market square with Vita beside him. He still looked cheerful, so she persisted.

'But Llewellyn is not likely to have settled for that. I guess he would want to interview someone in authority at the college too. A senior tutor, a chaplain, someone like that.'

She looked at White to catch any change of expression. There was none. His features betrayed only mild neutrality.

'You would have been present. I wonder what a senior tutor would have said to change Llewellyn's mind completely.'

White stopped. They had left the market and were close to the police station now. 'Nothing,' he said. 'He said nothing.'

'Longbridge's senior tutor said nothing?'

'Nothing is exactly what he said. There is no harm in telling you that. The Inspector, in his office, asked the Senior Tutor whether he could offer a character reference for Mr Henry Longbridge.'

'And what did he say?'

'Nothing. He said nothing. Literally nothing. The gentleman from Pembroke sat there and made no reply. Not a word. He just sat there in silence. I waited. My pencil was in the air, ready, but he did not answer. The silence grew longer and longer. Plainly the tutor was not willing to give Longbridge a good character reference, but he was not willing to say anything bad about him either. Either way, the silence alone was enough. He left without uttering another word. I wrote *long silence* in the notes. I didn't know what else to write. Llewellyn ordered Longbridge arrested that same afternoon.'

'So the college wouldn't say a word against him, but not saying a word was enough! That's astonishing!'

White walked on, leaving Vita on the corner by St Andrew's church. 'I told you nothing, remember,' he said.

'Yes. You told me nothing. Thank you, Constable.'

He waved over his shoulder. 'It was nothing,' he said.

VITA TURNED and walked back to the market and through the crowds to the Senate House noticeboards. Was it possible that she had missed her own name?

Apparently so. There it was, third from the top: *V. Carew, Newton College.*

CHAPTER 36

*T*he atmosphere at Eden Street could hardly have been more cheerful. Having set out for Ely under duress, Vita's father had returned positively jovial. She found him admiring the kittens in box in front of the fire.

'Have you ever seen such dear little things, Vita? Just look!'

'How was the recital in the cathedral, Papa?'

'Sublime! Celestial! I would almost say divine! Yes, I would even go that far. And the building - well! The stained glass! The lantern. It is unmatched. I had quite forgotten.'

There was an air of self-satisfaction about Aunt Louisa, but she was resisting telling her brother that she had told him so. Instead she passed him a slice of seed cake and smiled over his head at Vita.

'The recital was extraordinary. To think of Mr Pottendale - grey, shy, nervous little Mr Pottendale - being able to release such power, such music from that vast and magnificent instrument,' she said.

'Was he hidden throughout?' Vita asked.

'Yes. Invisible in the organ loft. Just the way he likes to

211

be. It frees him to play like the genius he truly is, one imagines. He came down, afterwards and we congratulated him, but he only wanted to hurry away.'

'Extraordinary gifts!' Vita's father said. 'And you, my dear, what was the outcome of your meeting? You feared bad news, I believe.'

'I did, but …' Vita wondered how to tell him what had happened, but her aunt interrupted before she could start.

'You'll never guess who we met on the train, Vita? Miss Emily Shorto! Remember Miss Shorto, your teacher? She was in the same carriage. *Such* a coincidence! And we simply couldn't stop her from singing your praises, could we, Stephen? On and on she went, about your diligence, your application, your natural instinct for scientific work. We could hardly get a word in edgeways. She put it all down to your father's early training when you worked together on his moths, and so on, didn't she, Stephen?'

Her brother was holding a squirming kitten up to admire it more closely. Its eyes had not opened. It cried so loudly that Minmou looked over in alarm. Vita couldn't remember her father being particularly fond of kittens in the past, but he seemed spellbound by this one.

'Miss Shorto was very kind,' he said, stroking the little head with his forefinger. 'She made a good point, I thought. The earliest formation of a young mind does count for a great deal. I have always said so. She will not hear of your leaving your studies, Vita. She says it is out of the question. *A way must be found*, she said.'

'I may have found one, father, as a matter of fact. Or been offered one. It won't cover all my expenses, but it will help.'

'Miss Shorto,' her father went on, 'is even willing to tutor you herself at the lowest possible fee. Such generosity! I have never met a scientific lady before. I must tell you, I was highly impressed! She knew about architecture. She knew about Bach. A thoroughly cultivated lady, and most charming. If that is what the study of science can achieve, then I can only hope you follow her example.'

'A sherry, I think. To celebrate a thoroughly worthwhile excursion,' Louisa said, 'and the warm reception for Mr Pottendale's portrait. The Master has thoroughly approved it, and the college wants at least three more of the Fellows painted. I shall be busy until Spring!'

The odd suspicion crept into Vita's mind, as she held up her glass to salute the others, that somehow her aunt was one step ahead, as usual. As the sherry turned her nose red, she wondered whether the meeting with Miss Shorto on the Ely train really had been a coincidence. But someone handed her a sleepy kitten, which somehow banished further analytical thought.

THE TEA PARTY two weeks later was not to celebrate Henry Longbridge's arrest and remand to prison – that would be improper – it was to mark Louisa Brocklehurst's new commission: the full-length portrait of a celebrated philologist.

'I am happy to say that he is different in every way from my last sitter,' she remarked to Mrs Goodman over cucumber sandwiches. 'He is twenty years younger and really quite dashing! Flamboyant waistcoats, and so on. We have met only once, but he has already spoken most interestingly about his holidays on the Rhine. He plays the oboe.'

'Not while he is having his portrait painted, I hope!' Mrs Goodman said, laughing. 'I wish my dear husband would take up a musical instrument instead of inventing. We lost two more panes of glass in the conservatory to the Muscle Enhancer last week.'

'There will be one in every gymnasium one day,' her husband remarked.

'One what will there be in every gymnasium?' Aloysius Derbyshire asked, only having half overheard.

'I have invented a machine for strengthening the muscles of the arm through repeated flexing against resistant tension,' Dr Goodman told him.

'Have you? That sounds ideal for swordsmen. I would certainly like to test it at my establishment.'

Vita left the gentlemen discussing the Enhancer and took her tea over to sit with Adelaide on the sofa.

'Forgive me, Adelaide, but I have never asked what subject you're studying.'

'The best and finest subject there is,' Adelaide replied. 'The only subject really worth studying, in my opinion.'

'And that is…?'

'Assyriology, of course!'

'Oh! I did not expect that.'

'Nobody does. Assyriology is utterly fascinating and essential to the life of all mankind, but we keep it to ourselves in the department for fear of being overrun. We want to decipher the great texts in peace, not like the poor fashionable Egyptologists, overrun with sightseers and magazine reporters. I'm working on cuneiform at the moment. Marvellous! But an acquired taste, I admit. What about your scientific work, Vita? Is all well?'

'It was touch and go for a while. I struggle with physics and maths, not having had much schooling. I have a paid post now, in the post mortem lab, which will bring in enough to pay for some extra coaching.'

'Assyriology and dead bodies. Perhaps we both have odd

tastes. Do join me in your brother's Oriental Self Defence class. The other three young women all squeal and giggle – it's terribly annoying.'

'Perhaps I will.'

Miss Hazelton was gesturing to Vita from the other side of the room. 'I wanted to tell you, Dear, I have a new lodger, Mr Dawlish,' she said, when Vita went to her. 'He works in the Post Office. Rather a dull chap, after Albert, but pleasant enough. And willing to pay more.'

'And how is Agnes?' Vita asked.

'Agnes has decided to retire. Her mother needs her, and she has Albert's money now. I gave it all to her. We opened an account she can draw on. She has an odd fear of paper money.'

'You gave it all to her?'

'She needs it more than I do. Agnes has been pawning things to make ends meet for years. Some of them were my possessions, too, but she always brought them back, eventually.'

'You knew?'

'Of course.' The old lady smiled and brushed a cake crumb from her skirt.

'Would you still like to try climbing, Miss Hazelton?'

'I have left it a little late now, dear, I'm afraid.'

'My friend over there,' Vita said, indicating Adelaide, 'is an excellent climber. Shall I ask her to find a climb suitable for a senior lady who is also a beginner?'

'Do you really think she could?'

'Oh yes,' Vita said, 'I'm sure she could rise to that challenge.'

.   .   .

'GUESS WHAT NAME George has given his new kitten,' Mrs Goodman said, as Vita passed.

'He is to have one of the kittens? I thought there were too many mouths to feed already at number 139?'

Mrs Goodman rolled her eyes. 'The children mounted a full-scale operation. They visited the butcher and the fishmonger and secured promises of scraps for cat food. They made a basket out of an old hatbox, lined with an old scarf, and they salvaged two chipped saucers from the dustbin for its feeding bowls. Amy wrote a letter, which they all signed, begging for a kitten and promising to pay for everything the cat would ever need for its entire life, even if they had to borrow and repay the debt long into adulthood.'

She sipped her tea, shaking her head. 'When Charles came home from the hospital, they met him in the hall, silently fell to their knees, and handed him the letter, which incidentally said they would all have to go and live in the treehouse forever, if he said no.'

They both laughed. 'So what will Georgie call the kitten?'

'Robert. Bob for short. His sisters tried to make him change his mind, but he was adamant.'

TEN MINUTES later Adelaide and Miss Hazelton were making plans.

'Shall we start in the spring, once the weather is warmer?' Adelaide said.

'Yes, that would be best, I'm sure.'

'We shall need a programme of preparation, beginning with small ascents, to build strength and acclimatise. We can work up to something more ambitious. What would you like to aim for ideally, Miss Hazelton?'

'I should like to look down upon the clouds from above,' said the old lady.

'I suggest we start with the tower of Great St Mary's,' Adelaide told her. 'The stairs are a pleasant climb. You will not be able to look down on the clouds from the top, but there is a good view of the city in clear weather.'

Miss Hazelton's eyes shone with pleasure at the prospect. 'And after that? Where should we climb next?'

'After that, the Gog Magogs. We can get there by cab, see the whole of Cambridge spread out below us, and be back in time for tea.'

'Oh, yes, dear, that would be delightful!'

'Then perhaps the Lake District,' said Adelaide, 'or Wales. Mount Snowdon, even.'

'Snowden! Yes indeed!' Miss Hazelton clapped her hands. 'And after that, my dear?'

'Well, after Snowden, the Alps are ours for the taking, I should say,' Adelaide told her. 'Which peak do you fancy?'

'The Matterhorn, I think,' Miss Hazelton said, and raised her teacup in celebration.

Poison at Pemberton Hall

A dazzling diva. A glittering society dinner. A servant with a terrible grudge.

Bookish, bespectacled Vita Carew longs only to be in her room pursuing her study of science. Her aunt has other plans, and insists they go to a gala dinner at Pemberton Hall, home of a girlhood friend. An internationally celebrated and glamorous German opera singer is to perform, and the grandest of company will enjoy a sumptuous dinner marking the household's return to high society after a terrible run of misfortune.

But disaster strikes as soon as the seafood is served. Vita can only offer first aid as elegant guests fall suddenly ill on all sides. Worse still, she suspects a death has been covered up to avoid interrupting the carefully planned soirée.

Vita must probe dark secrets behind the country house's elegant facade to work out who is to blame. But can she do so in time to prevent the poisoner striking again?

Wit, drama and a hint of the Gothic, if you like stylish mystery with your Downton Abbey, dip into Poison at Pemberton Hall today.

A Thin Sharp Blade

Shortlisted for the Crime Writer's Association Debut Dagger Award in 2019.

Cambridge 1903. Snubbed by male students and professors alike, Vita longs to study science but can only borrow books and work alone.

When a popular boxer dies and her brother collapses after an exhibition match, she spots a connection the experts have missed.

The very professor who brushed her dreams aside is the one she must convince.

Can Vita, with the help of a secret society of women students, an energetic swordsman and a strange lady photographer, convince the experts she is right and prove what really killed the boxer?

And how will the glamorous widow react?

A splendid bit of Gothic-tinged fun.

A witty mystery with a feisty heroine and irresistible period touches.

Slip A Thin Sharp Blade into your handbag today!

Dr Potter's Private Practice

A mysterious victim. A heartless doctor. An assistant whose loyalty extends to murder.

Christmas 1904. Falling behind in her first year of science, Vita plans a vacation devoted to study, but is lured from her books when a man with no memory is brought to the hospital, injured.

Curious to learn more, she retraces his steps to a disused well, but how did he get there? Piece by piece events leading to the attack emerge, revealing a long-standing arrangement between a country doctor and his wealthy clients.

Can Vita protect the amnesiac patient from the toxic partnership of the doctor and his dangerous assistant? Can she escape herself, and convince the police to investigate so many convenient deaths?

If you enjoy an Edwardian English Christmas with an extra frisson of gothic intrigue, Dr Potter's Private Practice is definitely one for you.

and available for pre-order soon

The Killing at Crowswood Castle

ACKNOWLEDGMENTS

Big thanks to my trusty team of early readers, proofreaders, editors, checkers and general supporters whose work is invaluable in bringing the books together. They are eagle-eyed and sharp critics, but it emerged this time that they are also a bunch of softies. After a first draft reading they were universally agreed that Georgie *had* to have a kitten! There was plenty of more technical feedback, but everybody agreed on the kitten.

What could I say? I gave in.

Thanks to the readers of all the Vita Carew titles, especially those who take the trouble to contact me with their views. Several want to see more stories that include Dr Julius Zecker, the German doctor from Poison at Pemberton Hall. Early readers of The Painted Penny Stamp are appealing for more of Coriolanus Long, the slightly dodgy ex-forger. I rather liked him too. (But then I would.) What do you think?

Fran Smith
May 2022
fran@fransmithwriting.co.uk

AFTERWORD

The lives of Edwardian women continue to be a particular fascination. I try to capture some of the barriers they faced in achieving an education, or even, like Miss Hazelwood, being allowed to risk going up a mountain.

Adelaide Robinson is an example of one of the daring young women of the period (and there were plenty of them) who simply acted as if there were no barriers in their way at all. Incidentally, there really was a volunteer fire brigade at Girton College. I recommend the Google images of them posing proudly with their ladders and ropes.

The idea of a painted stamp came from someone I met years ago, who had an annual challenge with a fellow artist. Each would attempt to slip a letter with a hand painted stamp past the Post Office's sorting system once a year. It seems an old-fashioned idea now.

Night climbers still exist in Cambridge. At Christmas you can often see a Santa hat on an otherwise dignified statue high up on one of the colleges.

Fran Smith

May 2022

Printed in Great Britain
by Amazon

39172405R10128